DEATH AND LETTERS

DEATH
AND LETTERS

Elizabeth Daly

FELONY & MAYHEM PRESS • NEW YORK

All the characters and events in this work are fictitious.

DEATH AND LETTERS

A Felony & Mayhem mystery

PRINTING HISTORY
First edition (Rinehart): 1950
Felony & Mayhem edition: 2015

ISBN: 978-1-63194-072-9

Manufactured in the United States of America

Printed on 100% recycled paper

Library of Congress Cataloging-in-Publication Data

Daly, Elizabeth, 1878-1967
Death and letters / Elizabeth Daly. -- Felony & Mayhem edition.
    pages ; cm
"A Felony & Mayhem mystery."
ISBN 978-1-63194-072-9
1. Gamadge, Henry (Fictitious character)--Fiction. 2. Book collectors-
-Fiction. 3. New York (N.Y.)--Fiction. I. Title.
PS3507.A4674D4 2015
813'.54--dc23
                    2015032042

CONTENTS

The icon above says you're holding a copy of a book in the Felony & Mayhem "Vintage" category. These books were originally published prior to about 1965, and feature the kind of twisty, ingenious puzzles beloved by fans of Agatha Christie and John Dickson Carr. If you enjoy this book, you may well like other "Vintage" titles from Felony & Mayhem Press.

For more about these books, and other Felony & Mayhem titles, or to place an order, please visit our website at:

www.FelonyAndMayhem.com

DEATH AND LETTERS

CHAPTER ONE

Crossword

THERE WAS A ROW of narrow casement windows across
the east end of the bedroom, and a sash window, broad and
high, in the north wall. The middle casement window was
partly open, the sash window shut tightly and screwed down.
To the north old trees, barely in leaf, screened the view
up-river; to the east the grounds were cut sharply off where
the cliff ended. A pale, cold April light, subdued by grey skies,
came into the room bleakly. It was a comfortable, almost a
luxurious room, but it had a clumsy, cluttered look to modern
eyes; it was old-fashioned in an unfashionable way. It had an
oriental rug on the floor, a gilt-framed oil landscape over the
chimney piece, thick silk curtains, pottery lamps with silk
shades, ornate wooden furniture, a double bed. Logs burned
in the fireplace—it was a cold afternoon.

A nurse in uniform sat beside the north window, doing a
jigsaw puzzle. She was a squat, dark woman, and the sharp lights
from her cap and dress brought out greenish tints in her sallow

skin. She had the bulging forehead of obstinacy, and there was strength in every motion of her short arms. She must have known that she was not much to look at, and perhaps she thought that that was why her patient sat with her back turned; perhaps that was why she cast a sour look at the patient's back, now and then.

The patient had moved her little bandy-legged desk from under the casement windows to the corner next to them on the right; it was now under a looking-glass in a painted velvet frame. The patient had said she got the light better that way, and certainly she must have needed all the light there was for her eternal crossword puzzles. She was doing one now, out of a little paperbound book. There were printed forms and business envelopes on the desk-flap, but she had pushed them and the ink and pentray aside.

She seemed to be making heavy work of her puzzle just now. She filled in squares, rubbed out letters, consulted other diagrams in the book, sat in thought, looked up often at the mirror, which reflected the top of the nurse's cap.

She was perhaps forty years old, and she might once have been a beautiful woman; now she looked pale and worn. She was very thin. Undoubtedly she had had an illness. But her dark hair was carefully dressed, and she was very neat and smart in plain black, with thin black silk stockings and black suède shoes.

The nurse said: "Don't tire yourself out, now, Mrs. Coldfield."

"No."

Mrs. Coldfield watched the cap in the looking-glass, but it wasn't moving. She filled in the last blanks of her puzzle; with dots substituting for the black squares, it looked like this:

THEMA.PLESCLIFF
S.I.D.E.T.H.I.R
DFLOO.RBACKFROM
W.H.A.TCFENWAYH
ASTOLDMEITHOUGH
T.Y.O.U.M.I....

GHTIMAGI.NESOME
W.A.Y.T.O.G.E.T.
MEOUTO.FTHISPLA
....C.E.Q.U.I.E
TLYIDONOTSEETHE
E.N.D.A.N.D.S.H
ALLNEVERH.AVEAN
Y.O.T.H.E.R.C.H
ANCETOCOM.MUNIC

She turned the thin page, and the nurse spoke again: "You going to do another? How they coming?"

The cap in the looking-glass was rising. Mrs. Coldfield turned another page to a half-finished diagram. She said: "Not very well. They're rather hard—for me."

The nurse had come across the room and was looking over her shoulder. She said: "I'd go crazy."

"They rest me."

"Only trouble, they're not sociable. How'd you like to help me with this jigsaw I'm doing? You can talk and do jigsaws."

"I'd like to go on with this for a while."

The patient spoke politely, but without expression. The nurse, disgusted, went down the long room and through a communicating bath to another bedroom beyond. The patient's eyes followed her. She came back with an open box of candy.

"Have one?"

"Not before tea, thank you."

The nurse went back to her jigsaw. Irritating, she thought, how she never calls a person by name; as if you didn't have a name or weren't there. But you couldn't irritate *her*...not if you tried.

The patient turned a leaf to an untouched diagram. She worked faster now:

..ATECONSULTDRD
A.L.G.R.E.N.F.O
RCASE.HISTORYON

L.Y.M.R.S.Y.E.A.
BLAGDONFO.RBACK
G...R.O.U...N.D.
ONLYNUR.SEHASSU
P.P.E.....R.A.T
EIGHTSY.LVIACOL
D.F....I.E.L..D

She glanced up at the mirror, carefully removed the two pages from the book, folded them once, and slipped a stamped, addressed envelope out from under the business papers on the desk. She put the crossword pages in the envelope, sealed it, folded it into one of the printed forms, and fitted both into a long envelope which was addressed in bold type to an industrial company in New York. Then she looked at her wrist watch. Still looking at it, she said in her quiet, expressionless way, "I had no idea it was so late."

"Late?" The nurse looked at *her* wrist watch. "Late for what?" she asked comically.

"The postman will be coming. I must sign these proxies and get them off. Date them, too; it says so." She picked up a card. "Date them. What's the date, I wonder?"

"It's Easter Monday," said the nurse, "April the eighteenth." She got up and came over. "You shouldn't be bothered with business."

"You heard my brother-in-law ask me to do them." The patient was signing busily.

"Is there any rush?"

"There is, by what they say."

The nurse was not likely to read the fine print on those mysterious cards and letter-sheets, and she accepted the probability that rush was a part of business. She stood while her patient blotted the forms and put them in their envelopes. When they were ready she picked them up and licked the flaps. The patient sat without looking at her, motionless—entirely motionless; she was holding her breath.

When they were all sealed, Mrs. Coldfield suddenly leaned forward with her elbows on the desk-flap and her head in her hands. The nurse stood looking at her sharply.

"You tired yourself out, just like I said. Now don't do another thing before tea."

"I hear him on the gravel."

"Such ears I never—you can't hear him all the way around to the front."

The nurse walked over to the door, was about to push the button of a bell, glanced back at the figure bowed over the desk, and raised and dropped her shoulders in a skeptical kind of shrug. She looked at the casement—a cat could get through that half-opening, nothing much bigger would make it. She went out, locked the bedroom door behind her, and descended two flights of stairs. When she came back the patient was sitting in an armchair, her head back, her eyes closed. She looked quite peaceful.

"Mustn't brood, you know," said the nurse brightly.

The patient opened her eyes slowly and looked at the other woman.

"Have to be cheerful to get well." The nurse switched on two of the lamps. "Tea's coming."

"Doctor Dalgren said I was well."

The nurse frowned heavily. "It's Doctor Smyth's case now."

"Of course. Silly of me."

"How about tea downstairs? Make a change." She added: "They're all out, every last one of 'em."

The patient smiled. "Yes, I know."

"That party at the Watertons', that ought to be something! Too bad you had to miss that."

"In any case I couldn't have gone. I'm in mourning."

The nurse, taken aback a little, said after a pause: "Well, it's only a family party after all. It's all right for them to go to that."

"It's all right to go to anything, if you feel like going."

"That's what I say. Come on now, take an interest; let's go downstairs for tea, and then out for a walk."

Mrs. Coldfield said as if in slight surprise: "But what if callers came?"

This was in bad taste, execrable taste. The nurse said stiffly: "They won't come in the library—Mr. Ira's little library." She added: "You're not well enough to see strangers."

"I can see that it wouldn't do."

"Now don't be naughty. I want to tell the doctor that you're ever so much better."

Mrs. Coldfield turned to look at the nurse steadily. She asked: "Well enough to travel?"

The nurse returned the look. There was a question in her eyes, too. But after a moment she said loudly: "Doctor Smyth is a very experienced man, he has a big reputation in this vicinity. All the big people have him, and he has ten times the medical knowledge of these psychiatrists."

Mrs. Coldfield leaned back again. She said: "I'll have tea upstairs, if you don't mind."

"I won't take hold of your arm."

There was a long silence. Then Mrs. Coldfield turned her head again, met the nurse's eyes, and smiled. She said: "If you did I should understand."

The nurse thought: She's a smart one. It's none of my business, Smyth knows his job. But what did she *do*?

CHAPTER TWO

Urgent

"**YOU MEAN YOU THINK** there's *anything* crazy about that letter?"

Gamadge's tone was flat and incredulous. He had not taken the clients' chair in his friend Macloud's law office, but had pulled up a hard straight one, and was sitting on Macloud's right, across the corner of the desk. He had taken his cigarette out of his mouth, and was pointing with it at some papers laid out on the blotter.

There was an envelope that had been through the mails; it was addressed to Gamadge in a firm, clear hand. There were two crossword-diagrams, one entirely filled in with pencilled letters, the other partially so. There was a typed, punctuated transcript of their message. There was a sheet of notepaper, covered with Gamadge's scrawled writing.

"Fifty-fifty," said Macloud, "but we have no evidence."

"No evidence..." Gamadge repeated the words without inflection. He put the cigarette back in his mouth and looked up at the ceiling, around the room, out of the window that gave him a large view of skyscrapers and April sky.

Macloud, with a saturnine look at him, picked up the typed transcript of the message. He glanced over it, and said judicially: "I've changed my mind. There's a distinct flavor of persecution mania—the odds from where I sit are two to one." He added: "Why not wait until Hamish reports, before we bet on it? You say he's calling this Dalgren for you. I'm willing to give you a break."

Gamadge said: "Just read it again."

"And you still have to see Mrs. Y. E. A. Blagdon, whoever she is. I'll give you Mrs. Blagdon, too." He added with amused curiosity: "I don't know how you wangled the appointment, in the face of your client's restrictions."

"I said Clara and I wanted news of Sylvia Coldfield." Gamadge looked at him disgustedly. "My client has a little more imagination than you have. Why don't you really read the thing?"

Macloud did so, aloud:

The Maples, Cliffside.

Third floor back.

From what C. Fenway has told me, I thought you might imagine some way to get me out of this place quietly. I do not see the end, and shall never have any other chance to communicate. Consult Dr. Dalgren for case history only, Mrs. Y. E. A. Blagdon for background only. Nurse has supper at eight.

Sylvia Coldfield

He put the paper down, leaned back, picked up his cigarette, reflected for a few moments in silence. Then he said: "Of course you did dig up a little something; but it's all in favor of my theory. Want a summing up?"

"Go to it. I'd like to hear it."

Macloud separated Gamadge's scrawled notes from the other papers, bent over, and frowned heavily. "Wish you'd type everything. Let's see. 'Ames Coldfield, kind of a literary character from what the book says about his clubs. Ira Coldfield. Mrs. Ira, born Georgette Soames. Glendon Coldfield. Mrs. Glendon, born Sylvia Haynes. Miss Susan Coldfield, belongs to the Ira couple.' All seem to live together at The Maples, Cliffside, which town as we all know is a little way up-river, west. This," he looked around at Gamadge, "means that your client is married and living in the bosom of her family. Sounds as if she were comfortably circumstanced. And she can send out letters—if you call that piece of mystification there a letter."

"She has no writing paper," remarked Gamadge, "and the envelope was mailed to me yesterday—Tuesday—in New York. From this neighborhood downtown."

"Somebody mailed it for her in New York," said Macloud patiently. "As for the form of her message, it simulates a code or cryptogram; but it isn't a code or a cryptogram, it's clear. Just a childish attempt to mystify, an attempt to impress you. And by gum she succeeded."

"She succeeded." Gamadge put out his cigarette and lighted a fresh one. He said: "She has a nurse on that third floor back, and you could fool a nurse pretending to do a crossword puzzle. The envelope is cheap grade paper, with no return address on it. Perhaps she stole it out of the nurse's box."

"And who mailed it for her? Well, that doesn't matter; we don't even know that she's sequestered up there. Dalgren, you tell me, is a top flight mental specialist, with a big rest home or institute up near Albany."

"Hamish told me when I rang him this morning. He knows all about Dalgren; he was perfectly willing to call him up for me."

"Speaking non-professionally, I'd say we didn't even need his report. She's been under Dalgren's care, she's back home and she's had a relapse. Delusions. Don't they always want to get away from wherever they are? It's a symptom," said

Macloud cheerfully. "She heard about you from Caroline Fenway, and she's elected you to help out with the charade. Speaking professionally, I wouldn't touch it with a barge-pole. Family affair—keep away from them."

A diffident, fuzzy-haired, youngish woman with an intelligent face came in with a memorandum slip in her hand. She said: "There's an Ira Coldfield in the telephone book, Mr. Gamadge; he's a broker, firm of Coldfield and Wittemore."

"Thank you, Miss Murphy." Gamadge looked at Macloud. "Hope you don't mind, Bob? I stopped by on my way in and asked Miss Murphy to look for a Coldfield when she had time."

"Fine," said Macloud. "That's the way. Get us all working for you."

"There's no Ames Coldfield listed, Mr. Gamadge, or Glendon either," said Miss Murphy, "but here's the Coldfield and Wittemore number."

"Oh, thanks," said Gamadge, taking it, "but what I really want now is a word with Avery Bradlock. He'll have all the information there is on brokerage firms of standing, and it wouldn't embarrass me so much to ask him."

"We mustn't embarrass the guy, Miss Murphy," said Macloud. "Get him Bradlock."

"Right away," said Miss Murphy, and went out wondering what was so attractive about that Gamadge anyhow, he wasn't good-looking and he had a kind of a stoop in the shoulders too.

The telephone buzzed in a minute or so, and Macloud gestured for Gamadge to take it. Avery Bradlock said it was very nice to hear from him, what could he do?

"Something came up in the course of business, Mr. Bradlock; I wondered if you could give me a little information about Ira Coldfield, of Coldfield and—"

"Wittemore."

"Yes. I wouldn't bother you with anything I could get out of Bradstreet, of course…"

Bradlock laughed. "I don't know much more than that, but that everybody knows. It's a very old well-established firm; Ira has a seat on the Exchange, and so did his father and grandfather before him. The grandfather—Deane Coldfield—was a sharp operator in the old days, but they're conservative now. Steady people, they've weathered everything. I wouldn't say they make a lot of money now, but who does? They get along. Ira's liked on the street, but I always found him—this is confidential?"

"Absolutely."

"Over-cautious man in every way. I suppose I don't like it in him because I'm inclined to be that way myself. You can't relax with Coldfield."

"What's the brother like?"

"Glendon? He's dead."

"Oh." Gamadge glanced at Macloud, who was listening in.

"Quite recently, too; was there some accident or something? I could find out."

"Don't think of it. So can I."

"He was a very nice fellow, not a bit like Ira. Easygoing, didn't much care whether school kept or not. He was on salary in the firm. They all got something from the father's estate, and I think his wife had a little money of her own, so he was more or less independent and didn't have to dig at it."

"Well, I'm greatly obliged, Mr. Bradlock."

"Not at all. Hope we'll be seeing you and Mrs. Gamadge."

Gamadge put the telephone down gently. He said: "She hasn't quite as much family as we thought."

"No," admitted Macloud, "but this cool cautious Ira doesn't sound especially sinister to me. And whatever they're doing or not doing to Glendon Coldfield's widow, they're evidently not going to get much money out of her."

Gamadge said: "My client has lost her protector; she's living among her relatives by marriage." He bent forward and drew the crossword diagrams towards him.

"Nice choice of words she has, don't you think so, Macloud?"

Macloud raised his eyebrows.

"These pages came out of an English crossword book," continued Gamadge. "London *Times*, *Sunday Times*. I had one.

They're tricky, and they require not only concentration and reasoning powers, but what amounts—for an American—to almost total recall. I mean the allusions wouldn't be familiar to just any of us—streets, place names, cricket terms, politics. If Mrs. Glendon Coldfield likes to do these puzzles, she isn't flighty or ill-informed or short on logic."

Macloud interrupted: "Things can happen to a good mind, Gamadge."

"Let's see how she uses her mind now, what's left of it. She had to compress her message into the space of two diagrams, because it couldn't take up much room. I don't know what that conveys to you; to me it means that my letter was probably an enclosure—enclosed in something she *could* send out. It was sent out on Monday, reached New York yesterday, and was forwarded on to me. Perhaps whoever found it enclosed thought it was there by accident."

Macloud said: "You're getting ahead of me."

"I am? She says she won't have another chance to communicate. That means that on Monday there was some combination of circumstances that will never be repeated again—in time. Surely one of the circumstances was a chance to send out a letter?"

"You're assuming—"

"I'm assuming that she's in her right senses. She gives me all the information she can, in few words: her address, the situation of her room, the one time of day when the nurse isn't with her. She knows and says that the job she wants me to do is difficult; she freely supplies me with the information that she's been a patient of Dalgren's. She implies that I'm welcome to what he can say. She gives me what I suppose is a social reference, Mrs. Blagdon. But I'm not to involve them in this attempt at escape—I'm to act quietly."

"Yes," said Macloud. "That's the catch. Why not inform Dalgren?"

"We don't know. But if Caroline Fenway had been here—she's in Europe with her father—I think this message would have gone to Caroline. They're intimate friends, or Caroline would never have talked to her about me—that business wasn't the kind of thing Caroline Fenway discusses with everybody. And they're alike in one thing, anyhow—no publicity. Mrs. Coldfield won't appeal to the law or the police, even if she can reach them."

"You still assume—"

"Just look at the understatement here, Macloud," said Gamadge. "It's a chilling touch—*I do not see the end.* The more chilling in that she puts it so quietly. She's up there in her third floor back, with the nurse, and she doesn't know what's being arranged for her downstairs."

"You're letting your imagination run away with you. If she's back from a sanatorium, and she's had a relapse, the family can't let her rave over the telephone to people, or"—he pointed at the diagrams—"send out such messages as that, or jump out of the window."

Gamadge sat back and smiled at him. "Yes, we've heard about such things; we read about them all the time. Somebody depressed; nurse turns her back, and the patient is out of the window. It's a perfect set-up. Who'd ask questions? Is that what she means in this message?"

"She's certainly sold you on it."

"She's certainly made me feel that it's urgent."

The telephone buzzed. Macloud listened, said: "Yes, put him through," and handed the receiver to Gamadge.

Gamadge, holding it turned down, asked: "Want me to take it in Miss Murphy's room? So you can listen in?"

"I can listen here again, if you'll hold it right." He moved nearer.

"Hello, Hamish," said Gamadge. "Didn't expect to hear from you so soon."

Dr. Ethelred Hamish was calm and deliberate in speech as in action, in or out of the operating room. He said: "Doctor Dalgren is to be found where he belongs, on his own premises. So is Bob Macloud, I presume. Is there going to be a lawsuit?

I told Dalgren, as you wished, that the information was to be used, if at all, strictly in Mrs. Glendon Coldfield's best interests."

"That's so."

"Well, I'm rather glad Bob's at your elbow."

Macloud leaned forward to ask: "Would you be glad to know that Henry's elbow is in my ribs, Red?"

"In a way, yes. You apply the brakes to him, and he balances the law's delay. Where was I? Oh yes, the story. I'd better give you the whole thing, otherwise you wouldn't quite understand about her. She seems an exceptional person."

"I'm sure," said Gamadge.

"Did I mention her by name? Very wrong of me. I shall refer to her after this as The Patient."

"There's a good deal of business in this office," Macloud reminded him. "Nobody's listening in."

"How trustful you attorneys are. Well: that family lives under one roof for most of the year now, for economy or convenience or out of pure affection, I don't know. It's quite a mansion, Dalgren says. The couple you're interested in did a good deal of travelling on and off—he was on salary in a family business, and had rather an easy time of it. He and the patient were devoted to each other—wrapped up. Very congenial.

"On Sunday, January thirtieth of this year, he—the patient's husband—was suffering from a recurrent attack of sinus; the attacks came every few months and were severe. Lasted for several days and kept him awake. His doctor here in New York—man named Goodrich—worked out an arrangement with him about sedatives. Man didn't like them, didn't like the way they made him feel. But after several bad nights, when he needed a clear head for business, he took one good dose of amytal, five grains.

"He wanted a clear head on Monday the thirty-first, so on the Sunday night he decided to take his five grains and go to bed early. He was taking the capsule in lemonade—thought liquor might not help his headache. The lemonade was sent up at nine, and his wife shut him into his room—they had a suite, two rooms and bath—and left him to his rest. Now don't get impatient, you ought to have the picture."

"I'm not impatient," said Gamadge. "I'm hanging on your every word."

"Good. In the morning he was found dead—overdose. He'd been given a box of six on Goodrich's prescription, and the box was on his bedside table, empty. His wife didn't think he'd had any out of that box before. He may have taken the whole six, therefore, but less would do the trick—four, in fact. There seemed no reason for suicide and many reasons against it, and the doctor up there—Smyth, his name is—fixed it up to be called an accident. But it looks as though it must have been deliberate.

"Just one of those mysteries. It pretty well killed his wife, she was stunned—and it was very tough besides, not knowing why on earth he wanted to go. But Dalgren says she has lots of character. Be that as it may, on February the tenth she seems to have repeated the pattern—took an overdose after or with her supper, and if a maid hadn't found her within half an hour she'd be as dead as he is. But Smyth luckily lives near them up there, and after a fight of it he saved her. But it was touch and go.

"In a day or two she was moved up to Dalgren's place— you can see why. She must have done it in an acute depression. She stayed two months, and Dalgren says he never saw anything like the way she came around; he never knew a more reasonable, better-balanced woman. Still grieving about her husband, but not morbid. She coöperated in every way. Only one queer thing, though. When she was able to have her first talk with Dalgren, and asked what had happened and why she was there, Dalgren says he could have sworn she didn't know. He didn't mention suicide, of course, wasn't ready to, just said she'd had an overdose of her sleeping medicine. She said she hadn't taken any sleeping medicine. But the empty box was on her bedside table. Of course she might have been covering up—some people do after a failure of that kind—or she might just possibly have blacked out on it and forgotten the whole thing. Nobody knows what can happen in such a case. I haven't much knowledge of psychiatry myself, but delayed shock can act in funny ways."

Gamadge asked: "Why did *she* have a box of amytal capsules?"

"Oh—didn't I say? When she got the prescription for her husband Goodrich doubled it so that she could take the other box along with them to Europe. They were planning a trip. Goodrich backs her up, by the way, on one point—she never so far as anybody knows took sedatives; never needed them.

"Mind you, after she denied taking amytal she didn't get excited about it or protest; she just let it ride. Trying to put the whole thing out of her mind? Dalgren says she improved steadily, even seemed cheerful when she was with other people, played bridge and walked. She evidently had lots of friends and interests, and he'd stake his professional reputation she was normal when she left."

"Has he heard since?"

"Not a thing. He recommended the usual—plenty of exercise, cheerful company, travel, some kind of work or hobby to keep her interested. I know how you laymen like labels; get it out of your head that she was ever insane. You don't, I suppose, think that attempted suicide necessarily implies insanity?"

"No."

"Tell Macloud to let her make a will if she wants to."

"Well, Red, I'm infinitely obliged. Oh—do you know any details about the way she happened to be found in time—after she took the stuff that night?"

"Matter of fact, Dalgren told me. It was Thursday, and the regular upstairs maid was out. The kitchen-maid brought up the tray. She wasn't up to much that evening, and she asked for some light food, soup and salad, and fruit for dessert. And cocoa. The kitchen-maid brought it up to her in bed, all but the fruit. When she came back with the fruit, the patient had only taken soup, and was lying back against the pillows asleep. The maid, tiptoeing out, dropped her tray and some dishes with a hell of a crash. She looked to see if she'd scared the patient out of her wits, but the patient hadn't moved an eyelash. Then the maid saw the empty capsule box, and remembered the other business. Tried to wake her and couldn't, yelled the house down. Smyth found amytal in the soup."

"I see. Thanks again, Red, and I'm sorry I can't explain why I was interested."

"I didn't ask any questions."

Gamadge replaced the telephone carefully, and looked at Macloud. After a silence Macloud said: "They don't know everything."

"I'm thinking of that set-up I mentioned. Why didn't they consult Dalgren?"

Macloud rolled his cigarette in his fingers. He said: "I could make contact legally, one way or another. Is that what you want?"

"Could you do it quietly? And at once?"

"It needn't be noisy; it couldn't be a secret. All depends on how her people react."

Gamadge rose. "All I want is for you to represent her if she needs a lawyer."

"Don't know why I shouldn't promise that. She certainly doesn't seem to be getting what the doctor ordered. But why don't *we* consult Dalgren?"

"She doesn't want anybody consulted."

Macloud looked up at him, frowning. "You'll be taking a fearful responsibility, Gamadge."

"I only wish I knew how to take it."

CHAPTER THREE

Letter Answered

GAMADGE STOOD IN FRONT of Mrs. Blagdon's Class A apartment building, and admired it; just far enough uptown, just far enough away from the avenue, fresh as the April day from its ivied terraces to its blue-and-white canopy; the blue of the canopy and its silver rods were picked up by the buttons and the uniform of the well-groomed doorman.

He went into a black glass and white marble lobby, where another man in uniform came forward to announce him. But when Gamadge asked for Mrs. Blagdon, the attendant showed what seemed strangely like reluctance. This was adequately explained within a moment of his taking the house telephone off its hook and getting into communication; Gamadge felt as if they had both instantly been whirled into a zone of furious activity.

"Mrs.—yes, Ma'am," said the attendant, his brow furrowed and his free hand clenching and unclenching itself at his side. "There's a Mr.—yes, Ma'am, they came. No Ma'am, I sent those back, but—the piano. There were seven boxes of—she didn't have the—it's red...Mr. Gamadge is—I said Mr.—no, the upholsterer couldn't..."

Gamadge said, laughing, "Why don't I go up? She expects me."

The man hadn't even time to answer. He gestured vaguely behind him towards the elevators, and an elevator man who had been listening with some sympathy accepted Gamadge as a passenger and took him up to the fourteenth floor.

"She just came back again," he explained as they rose. "It's always like this when they just get back."

"From Florida, I suppose?"

"Oh, that was all over long ago," said the elevator man. "She came back and went away again, south but nearer home. In a little while she'll be getting off to Europe, though."

He stopped the car and opened the door on a small lobby, decorated with something from Mexico, something from Florence, something from China. Gamadge pushed a button beside the only door in sight, and the elevator man waited to see whether he would be passed in. A calm-looking maid took his name and passed him in, and he was shown into a big, bright, modernistic room. A gleaming metal statuette on a thin column met his eye, but he couldn't approach it for the boxes and paper strewn on the hardwood floor.

His hostess appeared from somewhere with a rush, her hand out and a friendly smile on her pink-painted mouth. She was tall and rather large, with straw-colored hair rather wildly done, a white, translucent-looking complexion shadowed faintly here and there with bluish-mauve, and cloudy pale-blue eyes. The high style of her clothes was so far beyond the common that they seemed odd and a little mistaken.

She said: "Mr. Gamadge, this is so good of you; now I do hope *you* have something to tell *me* about dear Sylvia Coldfield, because I really know nothing at all except that she was very ill after poor Glendon—Walburg, we want something to drink."

The maid, who had waited for orders in the doorway, disappeared. Mrs. Blagdon had kept hold of Gamadge's hand, and drew him down beside her on a sofa. Gamadge couldn't for the life of him have said whether she was fifty or eighty.

"It's a shame I can't ask you to stay for lunch," she said with sincere regret. "But I have to go out. I've been terribly worried about Sylvia. I wrote from Palm Beach the minute I heard about Glendon—and wasn't that sad? Do you think he did it?"

"An accident, I heard."

"They always say so; and is it *ever*—but I mustn't say that. Why on earth should Glendon Coldfield—I've known the Coldfields forever, but I didn't know the wives so well. Charming, though. Georgette wrote back and said Sylvia was taking a cure. Then when I was in New York I tried to telephone, but I only got Ames, and of course he was sweet, he always is, but he said Sylvia was still keeping very quiet, and couldn't come to the telephone."

"That was our experience," said Gamadge. "My wife—"

"Have you tried lately? I haven't tried since I got back before. I've been so frightfully—"

The maid returned with a large open box of assorted flowers.

Mrs. Blagdon stared at them. "Put them...put them... Take them away."

The maid took them away.

"I was devoted to the Glendons," said Mrs. Blagdon, her eyes wandering back to Gamadge. "So intellectual. Not as intellectual as Ames, of course. Did you know he wrote?" The cloudy eyes expressed childlike awe. "Now Ira was my husband's favorite; he would be, both of them business men. As a matter of fact it was through my husband I first knew the Coldfields. Before dear little Susan was born, and now she's going to marry the Waterton boy—what a catch!"

"Those Watertons?" asked Gamadge respectfully.

"I should say so; they're neighbors up there. That's how it must have happened, I suppose; Susan is lovely, perfectly lovely, but—well, you know; she ought to be able to get anybody, anybody at all, but you know they don't."

Gamadge followed this without much difficulty. "The Coldfields haven't so much any more?"

"We all seem so poor now." Her eyes questioned his wistfully. "I don't mean they're really hard up; but those Watertons! Well, I'm so glad Susie got him. They were brought up together, of course, but that doesn't always work out so well. Does it?"

Gamadge said: "You had me worried for a minute there. I hope Mrs. Glendon has plenty to see her through this breakdown. Those things run into money."

"Well, of course Glen had his money from his father; Ira took on the business, and Ames put his share into an annuity. So sensible, but a little dull, I always say. And Sylvia has something of her own. Not much. It saves them all a lot to have the old place to live in—they were left it share and share alike, you know. Such a good idea, if people get on. I never can see why they can't."

"Nice that the Coldfields can."

"Well, they're such nice people. And the house is big enough—separate suites and everything." She added: "Gloomy old hole."

Several little grey dogs with bushy tails trotted into the room and circled it, pausing curiously now and then beside the heaps of litter on the floor.

"Siberian loulous," said Mrs. Blagdon, her eyes following them fondly.

"Loulous?"

"That's what the man said; I don't know how you spell it. I got them because it's such good exercise walking dogs—I ought to walk every day. It's wonderful exercise for me."

"I should think it would be." Gamadge was impressed. "All at once?"

"Oh yes, I drive up to the park with them, and—everybody talks to you. Every kind of person talks to you if you have

unusual dogs. So interesting. But four times a day! The vet said
so, and it seems excessive, don't you think so? But there are the
men downstairs, and I have my chauffeur."

Gamadge waited while the maid brought in a tray of
outsize old-fashioneds and canapés. She drove the little dogs
out of the room in front of her, and Gamadge and Mrs. Blagdon
raised their fat amber glasses and drank.

"Like the rest of us now," said Gamadge, "I'm hipped
about money. Did Glendon's share of the family fortune go to
his wife?"

"Yes, I know that much; my husband told me at the time.
I mean after Glendon lost so much on the market. After that
he tied up what he had left for Sylvia. But he didn't speculate
with his clients' money, I'm glad to say! My husband said so. He
simply hasn't the touch—hadn't, I mean. What fun Sylvia and
he had together— Winter sports and everything. It seems too
sad. No wonder she broke down. I offered to drive up and see
her, but they said not. I wonder if I could now? I might take
the loulous and give them a run."

"Big place, is it?"

"Oh no, just two or three acres running along the cliff.
Nice big trees, and there used to be gardens. I don't think
they keep much outside help now. Just one visiting gardener,
I think Georgette told me," said Mrs. Blagdon, enjoying this
subject and putting down her glass to give it her full attention.
"And no chauffeur. What did she say about the inside staff? I
met her at a cocktail party just before Christmas, and what
was it she said? They gave up their manservant. Cook, parlor-
maid and kitchen-maid is all they have to run that house with!
Well, some of them are always going away, so that makes it
easier. But you wouldn't catch me spending my money on
a place like that. However, they can't sell. Not for what Ira
wants, anyway."

Gamadge rose. "I can't tell you how much obliged I am to
you for letting me stop in, and for the drink and everything," he
said. "And it was such a pleasure meeting you."

Mrs. Blagdon again took his hand in hers. "I loved it. Wish I had any real news for you. When I get settled down next Fall I do hope you'll bring your wife."

"She'd be delighted." He added as Mrs. Blagdon half rose: "Now do finish your drink in peace. I can see myself out."

"Well then—and be sure you let me know what you hear, and then I'll tell *you*. I hope she's gone off somewhere; or if you get in touch with her, tell her she could come to me. Just for a little change, you know; I'd love to put her up, and she could be quite independent. It's so quiet here."

"I'll tell her—if my wife and I can make contact."

"If you just could!" Mrs. Blagdon gazed up at him with the anxious expression of one who is always trying to get somebody to take something off her burdened shoulders. "Make contact, and tell her, and everything. I'd be so grateful!"

"Don't worry about it."

"You are an angel; I'm so relieved. Say anything. *Make* her come. She needn't even write." That was certainly the last and greatest benefit—not to have to write.

Gamadge found a harried-looking chauffeur in the hall, rolling up a small rug. There was a distant playful snarling and yapping, and a voice from the back premises cried: "It was filly minions, and I said so over the tillyphone."

Gamadge, on his way down in the elevator, thought that Mrs. Blagdon's place wouldn't be the worst place in the world to get over a depression. He also felt a renewed admiration for his client; what a reference! Unprejudiced, disinterested and chatty, with no time to waste in asking questions. But as he turned into a drugstore on the corner, he felt baffled, puzzled and at a loss.

He went into a booth, called a number, and got an immediate response to his ring.

"Bantz speaking."

"Harold—thank goodness. Glad you didn't go out to lunch yet."

"Out to lunch, Boss?" Gamadge's ex-assistant was mildly surprised. "I went and came back."

"It's proletarian to eat so early. You have money in the bank now."

"It hasn't changed my appetite."

"I hope it hasn't changed your nature. Are you too much of a family man, stake in the country and all, for deeds of dreadful note?"

"What kind?"

"I don't quite know, but you're the only living creature I can ask. It may be no more than a scouting job. It may mean a little—er—interference. Just bring your avoirdupois along and take a ride with me tomorrow night."

"There's a little fat on me now."

"You can still walk? Run a little if necessary?"

"If necessary. I was going to work late here at the lab, but—"

"All the better, Arline won't miss you. I have every hope that we'll both come out of it alive."

"That's fine. Tomorrow, is it?"

"Thursday. It has to be Thursday."

"Something unusual about Thursdays?"

"You wouldn't know," said Gamadge, laughing, "but you may some time. I'll pick you up at your place, say at a quarter past seven. That suit you?"

"Suits me, but how are you going to swallow down anything in the way of dinner at any such hour? It's too late for you to change now. You'll choke."

"Shows you how important the mission is."

Gamadge, his face not so gloomy as it had been, left the store and took a taxi down town. He gave the driver an address in the Forties, sat back and lit a cigarette. He got out in front of an old converted brownstone house, with books in the second-floor window, and a small gilt sign: "J. Hall."

He climbed stairs, entered the outer room, and greeted J. Hall's clerk, the dusty Albert. Albert ushered him through into the sanctum, where J. Hall was having his ham sandwich and his whiskey and soda. A coal fire burned in the grate. J.

Hall was in the habit of saying that he was going to retire; he practically had retired, but still came to his office every day and spent eight hours there. Albert kept him company, sent out the few bills and circulars, and brought his employer mid-morning coffee, lunch and tea.

Gamadge said: "I won't sit down, Hall; just came in to ask a favor of you."

Hall, chewing, raised his eyebrows.

"I wanted you to let Albert make an out-of-town telephone call for me."

Hall swallowed, took a drink of whiskey, and asked: "Why?"

"I have to communicate with a client in code."

Hall sat looking up at him as if he couldn't believe his ears. Albert leaned against one of the folding-doors instead of shutting it, eyes on Gamadge, one hand smoothing back his mousy hair. Gamadge had taken a notebook and pencil out of his pocket, and seemed to be making notes with the calmest concentration.

Hall said at last: "Gamadge, you are a case of delayed adolescence. You will be kind enough to leave Albert and myself out of your pantomimes. If you actually have a code, use it yourself."

Gamadge looked up from his notes. "The opposition might check up on it; the code involves your having accepted an order—importation from England. But now the customer's dead, and you're calling to know whether you're to cancel or deliver."

Albert listened impassively; Hall seemed incapable of speech. When he spoke it was with restraint: "And why should I cancel, in those circumstances?"

"It would be the humane thing to do. Not a big bill—say twenty dollars or so."

"And the opposition, as you call it, will check up on us, and we're to maintain this deception or take the consequences?" Hall laughed shortly. "We have a reputation to lose here."

"That's just it," said Gamadge with incredible simplicity; or so it sounded to J. Hall—but Albert smiled. "Nobody'd question your bona fides."

"And now I'm to trade on it—after forty unblemished years in the rare-book business, which has its full complement of crooks?"

"There wouldn't be any consequences, Hall. I'm not getting you into trouble. They may check, though I doubt it; if they do, they'll leave it at that. In a day or so it won't matter—they'll drop it forever."

"So you say."

"It's a serious matter, Hall," said Gamadge. "Very serious matter for my client. Life and death, perhaps; or life and reason. I can make the call myself, and then you'll be able to say afterwards, if you like, that you didn't know anything about it. But I think Albert would be more convincing."

Hall had sat back in his deep chair, and his eyes were on Gamadge's. There was something in the expression of that old friend and customer that changed his truculent mood. After a long silence, he said without turning: "Albert, find out what this idiot wants, and do it—if it won't prejudice the business."

Albert came into the room. Gamadge said: "Albert, I want you to get this out-of-town number, and ask for Mrs. Glendon Coldfield. Give your occupation and this address, on request. They'll probably say that she can't come to the telephone; so then you leave this message: Mr. Glendon Coldfield's order has arrived from England. We have the crossword puzzle books, and the out-of-print novels; all the Shearings and that Chesterton—*The Man Who Was Thursday*. We now hear that Mr. Glendon Coldfield has died. Will Mrs. Coldfield accept delivery, or would she like us to dispose of the consignment? We may be able to do so. The bill amounts to about—"

"Twenty dollars?" barked Hall. "Twenty dollars? Are you out of your mind, Gamadge?"

"Some lucky bargains," said Gamadge mildly.

"And we can't fill any such order."

"I'll fill it—all but the crosswords, which got held up somehow and aren't in the package. But you won't be required to fill it. You can put in any trimmings you like, Albert; just what you'd say normally. Delay, slow going through the customs, and so on." He added, as Albert accepted the paper, "I'll be at your elbow."

"I guess it'll be all right, Mr. Hall," said Albert, who was not allowed to use the expression O.K.

Hall leaned his head back against the cushion of his chair. "Where's the code?" he asked with annoyance.

"I didn't dare put in the best part of it," said Gamadge gloomily. *The Passing of the Third Floor Back.*" He followed Albert into the front office. Albert was already calling Information. Gamadge hung over him while he got The Maples, Cliffside.

"Mrs. Glendon Coldfield?" asked Albert. A rather rough, husky female voice answered:

"This is Mrs. Ira Coldfield. Who's speaking? Mrs. Glendon Coldfield can't come to the telephone just now."

Albert droned: "Speakin' for J. Hall, Bookseller. I have a message here for Mrs. Glendon Coldfield—I'm Mr. Hall's clerk, in charge of orders."

"Oh," said the husky voice. "You can give the message to me. I'll tell Mrs. Coldfield. What is it?"

"It's this English consignment finally came in," said Albert. "There was a good deal of delay on it, and now we hear that Mr. Coldfield—Mr. Glendon Coldfield—died."

"Yes, he did. What's this consignment?" asked Mrs. Ira Coldfield impatiently.

"We have the crossword puzzle books, and all the Shearings, and the other out-of-print novels—the Chesterton, too—*Man Who Was Thursday.* You got that, Mrs. Coldfield?"

"Yes, I've got it. Are they paid for?"

"No, they had to pick them up, you know. Secondhand. Takes quite some time to locate those things, if you can at all."

"I suppose so."

"We got some bargains. The bill won't be much more than say thirty dollars. But Mr. Hall says to tell Mrs. Glendon Coldfield that if she don't care to accept delivery, we might be able to dispose of the lot elsewhere."

"Oh. You *could*?"

"There's quite a demand."

"Well, that's very nice of you," said Mrs. Coldfield. "I'd better speak to my sister-in-law."

"Have you a pencil, Madam? She might not remember what the order was; she might not know."

"That's all right," said Mrs. Ira Coldfield, still more impatiently. "I've got what you said. Hold the wire."

Albert looked up at Gamadge, put his hand over the receiver, and said: "She sounds dumb. We might put in that part of the code you left out."

"Better not," said Gamadge. "There are other people in the family, and they're not so dumb—or so I'm told."

The husky voice soon returned. "My sister-in-law says to thank you very much, but she'll accept delivery. Understands all about it. Make out the bill in her name. Goodbye."

"Thank you very much."

Albert looked up to find that Gamadge was smiling. He said: "Tell me the toll, Albert, and sell me a book. I'm in a buying mood."

All was proceeding merrily in the back room, with Hall urging bound sets and scarce copies on Gamadge, and Albert getting down plugs from top shelves, when the telephone rang. The three fell silent, and Gamadge and Albert looked at each other. They hurried into the front room, while Hall, leaning over the arm of his chair, scowled after them.

This time it was a man's voice with a finicking accent which came over the wire:

"Is this J. Hall's bookshop?"

"Yes, his clerk speaking," said Albert, looking pitifully up at Gamadge. "Mr. Hall isn't in."

"I just wanted to know—just a check-up," said the voice. "This is Mr. Ames Coldfield."

"Oh, yes, sir. I just had your—"

"Oh, did you? That's all I wanted," said the voice blandly. "My sister-in-law wasn't quite sure of the name of the shop. Now I myself know a little more about these matters; and I wished to be sure that this order *is* coming from your place. We didn't know about it, but that's nothing. My late brother had his own tastes." The speaker giggled.

"Yes, sir," said Albert, looking annoyed. "We imported the books for Mr. Glendon Coldfield. Have them up there—"

"No hurry," said Ames Coldfield. "No hurry at all. Thank you."

He rang off. The voice of Hall came from the next room. "I knew it. Whole family about our ears, and I don't even know the name of the misdemeanor. Or is it a felony?"

Gamadge said: "I don't know myself."

He walked home with a handsome if battered Molière, tall octavo, four volumes, half calf, Tome 1 missing, to find the lunch table set in the library, and Clara waiting for him.

"I'm in a kind of a jam," he said as they sat down, "about a friend of Caroline Fenway's. She's out of town, may be coming in tomorrow night; there might be reasons why she couldn't go to a hotel. Could we possibly put her up here for a night or two?"

"Miss Mullins wouldn't mind moving in with Young Henry for once," said Clara, "and her room's very nice since we did it over last Fall."

"Now you're in on it," said Gamadge, "and I'd better tell you the whole thing."

CHAPTER FOUR

Keep It Simple

THURSDAY EVENING was clear and cool, and the night would be cold; but there was a feel of Spring. Gamadge drew up in front of Harold's west side apartment house uptown, and Harold came down the steps and got into the car. If he had put on weight it didn't seem to have made much change in his stocky figure, and it certainly hadn't changed his dark face, which was as square and bony as ever and as lacking in expression of any sort.

He was never talkative. They had paid the toll on the George Washington Bridge, and were on their way again, before he made a comment; and that was after Gamadge had finished.

"Fenway again, for Pete's sake."

"Yes. We lost our client that time."

"Thursday means that maid goes out." He added: "That was a dirty crack. We got a regular sitter."

"More than we have."

"That Waterton the girl's engaged to—those the Douglas Watertons?"

"Yes."

"Whoo. They wouldn't want a scandal in that family."

"I thought the same. Makes it even stranger."

"Unless the client would be trying to make one?"

"I don't see it; or anything, yet."

"There are four of them besides her? And two men?"

"The one that checked up on Albert yesterday didn't sound physically formidable; but you can't always tell."

"How are you timing it?"

"If the nurse has supper at eight, that may mean that the family has dinner about that time. Our client may be with them downstairs."

"Unless she's locked up in the third floor back."

"We can't hope for such a break as that. If the pretense is that she's insane, they wouldn't leave her alone. The nurse wouldn't take the responsibility."

"Unless the nurse is in on it, and helping with the fatal accident."

"I don't think there'd be so many of them—doctor too—in on a fatal accident."

"I'll have to scout." Harold had had plenty of practice in that, and too much. He went on: "Let's hope she's on her feet, that's all."

"She wouldn't have put it up to me at all if she hadn't been."

Harold lapsed into silence. At a few minutes before eight Gamadge slowed the car to read the lettering on a square stone gatepost: THE MAPLES. There was another pair of gateposts farther north, and a semi-circular driveway led from one to the other entrance, past the recessed door of a stone house. A lantern hanging in the recess gave a minimum of light. All the front windows were closed, and light could be seen through chinks in the heavy draperies of the rooms downstairs.

Gamadge drove beyond the further gateposts, turned the car, and stopped it. Harold got out and walked on grass into the grounds.

Gamadge waited. He had two cigarettes and a period of uneasy thought before Harold came around from the south end of the house, crossed the lawn, and returned to the car. He leaned in at Gamadge's window.

"No lights upstairs," he said gently. "No lights in the garage. Front room on the left is the parlor—side curtains ain't drawn. Next to that, the library. Back of that a little kind of den, and the nurse is eating supper there. She's a toad type, and I'd hate myself to fight her in a hospital.

"There's a glass door out of that little den, kind of a French window. The back door is half glass, opens on a lobby, back stairs. The cook's in the kitchen, a nice big fat woman in a white uniform. The little kitchen-maid is in and out; she's all fixed up in frills to wait on table. She just got the dessert shoved to her through the pantry slide.

"The dining-room runs along from there all the way to the front; I got a good look in between the curtains on the last window down. It's a long room, as you can imagine, with the double doorway right up front and the table in the middle, opposite the mantelpiece. Extended, it could be seen from the hall; but now it's pulled in to accommodate six or eight. You can make it.

"They're all there, all five of them; you were right. Unless the fifth is company."

"Don't think they'd be having company nowadays," said Gamadge.

"I think she's our client; and she's the only one I couldn't get a look at in the face. She's sitting alone on that side of the table; dark hair done very neat and plain, dark kind of plain evening dress. They're all dressed for dinner. They're all talking but her. She's got her head bent down a little, just sitting."

"Waiting."

"I guess that's so. There's a big high-colored man at one end of the table, and a dressy woman at the other end."

"The Ira Coldfields."

"Good-looking girl and middle-aged man on the side opposite our client. The middle-aged man is talking away to beat the Dutch, face puckered up as if he thought he was funny."

"Ames Coldfield. Very intellectual." Gamadge added: "All right, let's go."

He got out of the car, and they went down under big old trees to the corner of the house, where shrubbery thickened. Harold stayed where he was. Gamadge rounded the house to the back door; he rang, and the stout cook looked out at him. He had not taken off his hat before she was smiling benevolently.

"I'm awfully sorry to bother you," said Gamadge, "but I had trouble with my car up on the route, and I wondered if I could telephone to a Cliffside garage. I don't want to disturb the family. Just when you must be serving up the dinner, too."

"I'm just sending in the coffee, sir. I have me own telephone here under the back stairs."

"I thought you would. Don't want to make a nuisance of myself."

She stood aside. "It isn't everybody would be so considerate. Come in, sir."

Gamadge entered a little lobby, with the kitchen on one side and a closed door on the other—the nurse must be behind it, eating, and Gamadge glanced at it with disfavor and apprehension. He went on to the telephone, beyond which a baize door shut off the front part of the house; the cook returned to her own premises.

He dialled without lifting the receiver, said a few words, and then walked through the baize door into the front hall. A broad hall, a broad stairway, then the lighted drawing-room on the right and the dining-room on the left. Ames Coldfield said something in a high voice, a woman laughed. Gamadge edged along past the drawing-room doorway; nothing was to be seen of the dining-room but a fine walnut console between the end windows, an oblong of Persian rug, side chairs against a panelled wall. He reached the front door and opened it a little way. Harold slid through, and was closing the door gently behind him while Gamadge went back as he had come.

He went through the baize door and on to the kitchen. The cook turned from the sink.

"I'm ever so much obliged," he said. "They're coming."

"You're welcome, sir."

He left the house, rounded it, and returned to the car. It started smoothly and quietly enough, and he drove down the curving drive to the front door. He waited, the engine running, and when the door swung open he was out of the car and had the rear door wide.

He had a view of three women coming from the dining-room, pausing, staring; he heard Harold's calm voice: "Car for you, Mrs. Coldfield," and saw him cut her off from the others as neatly as a sheepdog. He didn't have to touch her—she came out of the house like a sleep-walker, straight to the car and into it. Harold, right behind her, had slammed the door shut and was holding it.

Gamadge flung himself into the back of the car, Harold let go of the doorknob and tumbled behind the wheel. There was a double slam and they were off up the drive. They had almost reached the route before Gamadge got himself twisted around to look out of the rear window. A big man in dinner clothes stood only a few yards up the drive, and three other people were grouped behind him, like images.

"Gave them a surprise," he said, and couldn't help laughing. But he was surprised himself when he turned back to look at the passenger huddled in the other corner, and saw that she was laughing too.

It wasn't hysteria, although she gasped between fits of the laughter. She managed to speak: "It was so funny. So funny."

"It was, now you mention it."

"That man, that wonderful man. Who is he?"

"Bantz? He's a research chemist. Now don't let this kill you—he was a marine."

There was a certain wildness in her laughter now, and Gamadge said hastily: "Here, let me put this coat on you." He got Clara's topcoat around her shoulders. "And we'll have a drink. I need one too," he told her, filling the top of the brandy-flask. "It wasn't so funny until we put it through," he went on. And as she drank: "It wouldn't have been funny at all if you hadn't been magnificent. I never saw anything like the way you came through that door. Clockwork."

"But it was a car I'd been wanting so. I could never have got past the gates at any time without a car. And"—she looked at him, still smiling a little—"I'd had your message."

"Didn't that amuse you? I hoped it would."

"To think that Georgette gave it to me!"

"Your brother-in-law Ames checked up on us."

"He would; but it was only fussiness and wanting to be in on anything even faintly literary. He was amused by Glendon's choice of books. He thinks crosswords are very silly."

"I hope he'll know some day how silly they can be."

She had a silk evening bag on her arm. Now, opening it, she showed him the little paper-covered book. "Here it is. It was Glen's, but since he died I've been doing them too."

"How in God's name did you get the message out?"

"With some proxies."

"Of course! A business office would forward such an enclosure at once and as a matter of course—assume a mistake."

"It couldn't have happened again." She was sombre enough now. "They were all out, and the nurse wouldn't know that the proxies could wait. I wasn't allowed to seal anything; but she didn't look. I don't know how I—"

He said: "It's all right now. Have some more of this. The story can wait."

They had been going south at a fast clip; now Harold slowed, and grinned at them over his shoulder. "Time to get directions," he said. "Do we go straight back, pay toll and everything, or do we ride around by Jersey or somewhere? I mean are they coming after us?"

"No," said Mrs. Coldfield. "They won't come after us."

"You mean State Police won't even be waiting at the bridge to take a look at our passports?"

"No, once I got away it was too late."

"In that case," said Harold, stopping the car, "we might take it a little easy." He lighted a cigarette.

Gamadge asked: "Have some brandy?"

"Don't care if I do. Now that it's all over, I feel a little shaken."

"Some day, perhaps," said Mrs. Coldfield, "I can put it into words—what I feel. You mustn't think I suppose it was as simple as it looked."

"We always try to keep it simple," said Harold, handing Gamadge back the cup. "When I worked in the boss's lab we used to get things more involved sometimes. Now Plan One is always simple. I was afraid this time we might have to blow fuses, cut telephone lines—that's against the law, too—wrestle with the nurse. She looks as if she could break my leg. But the boss said we could probably depend on you keeping your wits, and you'd been warned, too."

He started the car. Gamadge said: "You've impressed him deeply. He doesn't talk much as a rule. Now about plans for the night. We could fit you out perhaps for a hotel, but my wife and I thought you might prefer to stay over at least until tomorrow with us. So far I'm an unknown quantity to your relatives, so they wouldn't know where to look for you. I don't want you bothered with telephone calls or visitors."

"It's too much to ask."

"Of friends of Caroline Fenway's? Of a man who's had the privilege of a sort of introduction to Mrs. Blagdon?"

"Dear old thing."

"You have an invitation to go there, too, but I think you ought to work up to that gradually, unless you feel the need for excitement right away. Besides, her intentions are excellent, but I don't think she could keep it quiet—your arrival without luggage as a refugee. I'm not sure her servants could. Now with us—you'll have to have the nursery governess's little room, but Clara seemed to think it would do. By the way, my wife can keep a thing quiet."

"I feel"—she had sunk back into her corner and closed her eyes—"so relaxed. It's the first time, since I came back to the house from the Dalgren place."

"You know, I can't see why you couldn't enlist the servants back there on your side. The cook seems such a nice woman."

She opened her eyes to gaze at him. "Cook?"

"I had to get in by the back way, to open the front door for Harold—never mind it now."

She closed her eyes again. "The servants were told that I was mad. What else could they believe, when a doctor and nurse said so?" She added: "I don't think the nurse believed it. As for Smyth, he's a poor silly old thing, devoted to them all. Perhaps he thought he was acting for the best. I could never make any fuss, you know." Her voice was so faint that Gamadge could hardly hear her. "I could never lose my temper or show resentment, I couldn't scream out of the window or try to burn the house down. That's the kind of thing they were hoping for."

"Were they trying to get you put somewhere for life, behind Dalgren's back?"

"I was afraid so."

"Were you afraid of anything more drastic?"

"Yes, sometimes. But Smyth wouldn't..." Her voice faded.

They were slowing for the bridge. Gamadge said: "Just try to rest now. We'll make one stop before we get to my place—don't wake for it. I'm going to telephone The Maples from a public booth."

She was startled. "Are you?"

"Mustn't leave them in a state of anxiety," said Gamadge, smiling at her.

"Mr. Gamadge—if you're going to talk to them, I must tell you that I gave them a hideous shock. They may *all* have been acting in good faith, except one. The whole thing is so frightful, I don't know how I shall ever tell you."

"Just let it go for now."

She was quiet. By the time the car entered the West Side Highway she was asleep, and Gamadge sat back watching her and smoking thoughtfully.

There was a drugstore on Harold's corner. Harold drew up at the curb, and Gamadge got out and went in. He called The

Maples; there was no waiting at the other end of the wire. A man's angry, frightened voice rasped: "Yes, who is it?"

"Am I speaking to Mr. Ira Coldfield?"

"Yes. Who is this?"

"A friend of your sister-in-law's. I wanted to tell you that she's—"

The voice shouted at him: "Are you one of the fellows that got into my house on false pretenses and got a sick woman out of the house and took her away in a car?"

"Would you call it an abduction?"

"You got into my house—the cook—"

"Your servants had nothing to do with it, Mr. Coldfield."

"I know that. You got in by fraud. I—"

"We were there by invitation. Isn't Mrs. Glendon part owner now? But let's not waste time discussing that kind of thing. We're quite ready to go to court if you are—produce her at any time. She has an excellent lawyer, and I'm sure Dalgren would testify. But you know your sister-in-law well enough to know that she dislikes publicity as much as you do—that's why we had to use the methods you say you object to, though I should think you'd be grateful for them."

"Does anybody want publicity in such a case?" growled Ira Coldfield. "I say you'll regret this bitterly—she was under a doctor's care."

"Not being mad ourselves, we—her friends—are quite willing to bank on Mrs. Coldfield's sanity. My idea is to come up there tomorrow and have an informal talk about the whole thing; and pick up some luggage for her, you know," said Gamadge amiably.

There was a silence, then a faint mumbling, and then a different voice—Ames Coldfield's—came thinly over the wire:

"This is Ames Coldfield speaking, Mrs. Glendon Coldfield's older brother-in-law."

"Yes, Mr. Coldfield?"

"Any friend of Sylvia's will be well received in our house, sir, and I wish that you had realized it before."

Gamadge couldn't help laughing. He said: "There seemed to be a little trouble about issuing the invitations."

"How I should love to know the procedure, but let's maintain a civilized approach, since you seem to be a civilized man."

"Thank you."

"The whole thing hinges on points of view—on what we thought and what you think about my sister-in-law's mental condition. You realize that, of course?"

"Mrs. Glendon Coldfield realizes that. She makes out a case for you."

"Of course she would. Sylvia is always fair—except where her delusions are concerned. Surely you can see that we would prefer to keep them in the family? Until she had abandoned them? But I agree with you, a conference is always best. No lawyers, of course?" He giggled.

"Only myself."

"Er—*you* are not one, by any chance?"

"Oh, no. A reputable lawyer wouldn't have used our methods."

Ames giggled again. "I'm glad you admit so much! Well, then: my brother is very much occupied, and tomorrow he won't be able to get away from his office and up here until shortly before six. Can you be here at six? We feel that it would be more satisfactory to have our whole family present at the conference, and three of us would have to make a special trip to town for it, and"—the giggle was prolonged—"you know the way."

"I'll be there. If you'll just get a bag or two packed for your sister-in-law?"

"I promise it."

Gamadge came back to the car. Mrs. Coldfield was still asleep, and Harold standing on the curb beside her window. He and Gamadge exchanged goodnights, and Gamadge drove off.

CHAPTER FIVE

Why?

CLARA SAID that Mrs. Coldfield probably ought to go straight to bed, that she had every reason to be a wreck. Mrs. Coldfield said that she had slept in the car and wasn't at all tired, and that she wouldn't be able to close an eye until she had told Gamadge all about it—she owed him that, at least. Gamadge said that he wouldn't be able to close an eye until he'd heard.

"But don't let that influence you," he added. "Sometimes I don't close an eye anyway."

They were in the office, which had once been the Gamadge family drawing-room; a high, long room, with a white moulded ceiling and a white mantel, beneath which a fire burned. Mrs. Coldfield was warming her hands at the fire.

She said: "I can't believe it—that I'm out of that house forever. It's very stimulating, Mrs. Gamadge, to be free; and not to be waiting. I'd rather tell the story tonight."

A big tawny chow and a yellow cat were sitting together near the wide doorway, paying close attention. They wanted to know when and where people were finally going to settle down. Clara joined them. She said: "In that case I'll be up in the library; it's awkward to talk to two. When you're ready, you'll find something to drink up there, and something to eat, too. I don't believe you had much dinner, Mrs. Coldfield."

"Not much; in the circumstances I couldn't eat much."

"Well, I'll be there with the animals."

But the cat Junior had other ideas; when Mrs. Coldfield sat down in one of the leather chairs in front of the fire, he ran over and sprang into her lap.

"Oh, leave him here," she said. "What a nice friendly one."

"He's rather officious, I'm afraid," said Gamadge. "He's trying to take Martin's place, the one that died."

"I wish they didn't have to die so soon. We couldn't have one at The Maples—Glen and I."

"He really doesn't bother you?" asked Gamadge anxiously, as Clara and Sun went upstairs. "We don't like to suppress him—he means well, poor little guy."

Mrs. Coldfield smiled at him as he sat down beside her in the other big chair and offered her a cigarette. "I don't think it will be so hard for me to tell the story as I was afraid it would be."

Gamadge lighted her cigarette and his own. Then he said: "Perhaps you'd rather *I* told it to *you*."

She turned to look at him.

"Think I couldn't?" he asked. "Think I don't know? By the way, the defense has tipped its hand: Ames Coldfield says you developed delusions, and that they were just keeping it all in the family until you got back to normal. So I said I'd go up tomorrow and get some clothes for you and have a conference. I said you have a lawyer, which is quite true—Bob Macloud, none better. But I promised not to bring him along with me, so we're all looking forward very much to the meeting."

She asked faintly: "A lawyer? I don't think—"

"Oh you needn't have him unless you need him. I just retained him so that I could say you had him; I think he's already made himself quite useful. Now for the story: and you must correct me where I go wrong."

Mrs. Coldfield's dark-blue eyes were fixed on his face; she nodded silently.

"We begin with your tragedy—your husband's death," said Gamadge gently. "A double tragedy for you, Mrs. Coldfield. The loss, and the unanswerable question—why?"

"He had no reason," she said in a muffled voice. "His affairs were in perfect order, we were happy. He was well, except for those sinus attacks; the doctor had looked him over just a little while before. We were planning the trip to Europe. Some day we were going to have a place of our own. Do you think I didn't know him? We'd been married twenty years."

"So you sank into a state of anxiety and depression," said Gamadge. "You knew it couldn't have been an accident."

"He never took more than one capsule at a time." Tears were rolling down her face. She wiped them away, and Gamadge said: "Do forgive me. It's part of the story."

"Yes. I know."

"Well, one night, worn out with all this, you went to bed early and had your supper brought up to you. You finished your soup. And the next thing you knew you were as sick as all hell, with people half killing you working over you."

"And then I was asleep again, and then I was in an ambulance."

"On the way to Doctor Dalgren's rest cure. For a while you were too exhausted and dazed to know or care what had happened, but at last the doctor told you you'd had an overdose of amytal. You knew what he thought; but strangely enough— all things considered—you shook off your depression, cheered up a good deal, and became a model patient. You didn't even bother to deny that you'd taken any amytal at all. Insist on your denial, I mean.

"You went home with Dalgren's blessing."

"I only meant to stay until I could pack up my clothes."

"But unfortunately for you, you didn't pack them up and go before you made your almost fatal mistake. You ought to have gone first, Mrs. Coldfield."

"I know that now." She turned her head slowly to meet his eyes.

"By Heaven," said Gamadge, "I wouldn't have waited to pack!"

"*You* believe my word—that I didn't take amytal?"

"Of course I believe you. And of course you had to warn them, but what possessed you, knowing what you did, to warn them on their own ground? Well, I can see it; you told someone whom you'd eliminated in your own mind. Very dangerous."

"I told Ames."

"Told him that since you hadn't taken amytal, it must have been given to you—in the soup. That the pattern *had* been repeated; somebody had poisoned your husband—put the stuff in his lemonade that night. Was that what cheered you a little at Dalgren's—the conviction that he hadn't committed suicide? It would be comforting, even if it implied murder."

"I didn't say murder, deliberate murder," she said, her voice trembling. "I said somebody had gone mad."

"Or *was* mad. Did you suppose that that would be pleasanter for them—with the daughter of the family engaged to a Waterton?"

"It was frightful, but I couldn't go off without telling Ames. He's very clever, and not at all sentimental; and he always seemed to like me, and he was very fond of Glen."

"None of that eliminates him, if he's a homicidal maniac. Had you any reason for thinking it was homicidal mania, apart from a natural difficulty in thinking of any of these people as murderers?"

"There wasn't any motive. I've been over it and over it," she said, looking away into the fire. "There simply wasn't any motive. We all got on well enough, Glen was a favorite. And his money, what there is, goes to me; and mine goes to some old cousins in Canada. If they'd died, I was going to make another will."

"What about your share of the house?"

"Glen sold out to the others years ago, reserving the right to come back and live there when we wanted to. But they could have sold at any time."

Gamadge sat back frowning. "The motive has discouraged me from the first. I couldn't make out what they gained from getting rid of you. But to tell you the truth, Mrs. Coldfield, I never much like the theory of an explosion of mania which you seem to have adopted; not when there have been no warning signals in advance. There were none?"

"Absolutely none at all, and there doesn't seem to have been anything out of the way—even eccentricity—in either family; the Coldfields' or Georgette's. But one does hear—"

"One hears of cooks poisoning whole families," said Gamadge. "Your theory did give the Coldfields an out—the servants."

"No, it didn't," she said anxiously. "The cook—imagine that nice Louisa doing such a thing!—she wasn't in the night Glen died, and the other maid, Agnes, wasn't in the night I was poisoned, and the kitchen-maid saved me."

"That's so." Gamadge said after a moment: "Four capsules made a fatal dose. So far as you know there were six in those boxes; six in each."

"There were six in the one I had; I'm pretty sure Glen hadn't had any out of his."

"So there may be another dose in somebody's possession, fatal as death. You thought of that, perhaps?"

"I told Ames I didn't dare to stay a night. I actually thought he'd understand; even that he'd sympathize."

"My poor Mrs. Coldfield, you were an outlander suggesting madness or murder to a member of the clan."

"I thought he did understand; he showed sympathy. That's the dreadful part of it. He said of course I must go if I felt as I did, and that he'd try to investigate—talk to Doctor Smyth. That was after lunch, in his little study. I went upstairs to finish my packing, and while I was at it the nurse walked in. I was never alone again afterwards, day or night. I couldn't go to a telephone, or write a letter."

"You had dinner with these people?"

"After they'd all talked to me, and were sure I wasn't raving."

"Their attitude was that you'd had a serious relapse, and had delusions, and that Dalgren hadn't understood the case?"

"Yes, that's what they said. At first they wanted me to retract—sign a statement that I had taken the amytal voluntarily. But after a day or so they never even pretended that I could go if I did that, the whole thing shifted—I was a danger to myself. Of course by that time I would have signed anything—I realized that they were going to have me committed somewhere. Georgette told me outright that it was too late, I wasn't responsible for what I did or said. It was no use repeating that I'd only wanted to warn them, and that I'd never say a word to anyone."

"You think some of them may have been acting in good faith?"

"I'm pretty sure some were. But one of them had tried to poison me, and might do it again, and the rest would certainly think then that it was suicide."

"You eliminated Ames Coldfield at first, or you wouldn't have brought your story to him," said Gamadge. "But you say you brought the story to him because he was intelligent and seemed fond of you and your husband."

She met his eyes. "Yes, I—"

"I repeat those considerations wouldn't eliminate him for a moment if your theory was homicidal mania."

"I only wanted to warn them and get away. Ames seemed—"

"Mrs. Coldfield, you know there's a better theory than that charitable one of yours. Can you really believe that a single Coldfield is a concealed maniac? Which of them would fill that bill?"

"I only thought of Georgette at all because she's nervous and high strung and takes violent prejudices, and because—I suppose because she never liked me very much. Susan—it's impossible, she's so happy. Ira hasn't a nerve in his body. Ames is utterly satisfied with himself and life, and he's amusing."

"In other words, all the Coldfields are sane."

"And I shouldn't have called Georgette anything else, if I had any choice at all."

"We'll cut out guess work," said Gamadge, stubbing out his cigarette. "We'll dig up a motive for murder somehow."

"There simply isn't—"

"You've only considered two motives—hate and gain. There are others. Let's draw on my dark experience."

"Mr. Gamadge, was that why you arranged to go up there and talk to them tomorrow? Because you thought—"

"I confess I wanted a look at them."

"But I told you—" she was distressed. "I only wanted to get away."

"You didn't warn the family against anybody but a maniac— whom they all know doesn't exist among them. You didn't warn them that there's a deliberate mass-murderer up there, and what's more, a poisoner—the kind of murderer that goes on and on; repeats the pattern, all right! It's too easy. How will you feel when it happens again?"

"Nobody would dare—"

"Wouldn't they! I'll tell you something for your comfort, though; just let one of those people get in a jam, or what they think of as a real jam, and they'll trip themselves up. You won't have to do it for them."

She smoothed the yellow fur of the cat sleeping on her knees. "Glen—one of them killed him. But they're his own people, and you may think of me as a fool if you like, but I couldn't hunt them down."

"Let them trip themselves up," said Gamadge, smiling. "Just give them a chance. Now let's see: the murderer certainly has a secret now; the motive was another secret. Who'd have one?"

She looked uncomfortable.

"Ames? No? Nothing serious, you think?"

"How could I know? I shouldn't say so. He talks about everything, even his silly past."

"Ira? An open book?"

"I'd say so."

"Susan? Wrapped up in her eligible and in her approaching marriage?"

"They're waiting until next Christmas. Jim Waterton is just starting in with his father's firm. Mr. Waterton wanted him to wait until he was earning a proper salary."

"The old illusion; let the young man pretend he's on his own feet?"

"They're very nice people; Jim is a charming young man. You must remember that Glendon and I were more or less outsiders—we were only there in the intervals. We used to take an apartment in New York for the Winter, but we were saving up for our own place, as I think I told you. This year we—"

"I know. You have no thorough, inside knowledge of these people's lives. How about your high-strung sister-in-law? Any secrets in *her* life, would you say?"

"It would be ridiculous of me to call them secrets. She does go around more or less on her own. Ira's too busy. She has her own friends."

"Enough said; let me do the rest of the sum in my evil mind. You see what I'm getting at, don't you? If your husband chanced on a secret—a disgraceful secret, a dangerous secret— would he keep it to himself and let the consequences take care of themselves?"

"If he said anything at all, it would be to the person. He often differed with Ira about things, but he didn't gossip even to me. He had it out with Ira, and Ira would be the one who talked—to Ames or Georgette. That's how I'd hear about it."

"What a liability a conscience can be. Let's theorize: he chances on the murderer's secret, and is killed. Then the murderer kills you, because you're supposed to have been told about it by your husband...no; that won't do."

"It won't?" He had her interest, no doubt about that.

"No, because you were allowed to live so long after his death. Wait a minute: we'll say he had evidence, and the murderer knew he had it. Any chance of a thorough search, with you in a communicating room?"

"No, none at all after his death. I was upstairs a great deal, and I never kept his door shut at night. Nobody came into his room at all, so far as I know. They'd only have a few minutes there if they did—we're on the top floor, with nothing else up there but the servants' rooms and an attic and store rooms."

"There you are, then. You had to be got out of the way."

She sat back, incredulous. "You mean somebody tried to kill me to get me out of the way?"

"Don't forget what I told you about poisoners—it's all so easy, they just repeat the thing that worked so well the first time. There you were, depressed—to the point of suicide."

"But there was no such evidence, Mr. Gamadge; I went through all his things. I meant to go—I wouldn't stay at The Maples without him. I was going south. I had to clear his things away."

"The thing wanted might have been a paper, a letter, something easily overlooked."

"I went carefully through his desk."

"And the pockets of his clothes?"

"Of course—I was giving his things away."

Gamadge reflected. "You didn't remove anything yourself?"

"I was going to keep some things; I hadn't removed them."

"A book?"

"He hadn't many in his room; I had most of ours in mine."

"Books would be the first thing the murderer would think of. And they wouldn't take long."

She said: "I only took the crossword book."

"The crossword book; oh yes, it was his, wasn't it?"

"It was one of the reasons I knew he couldn't have committed suicide. It was there on the table beside his bed, the morning I found him; with the pencil and a marker in it, and the puzzle half done. People don't do crosswords just before they kill themselves."

"No, definitely not."

"I brought it away; it was the last thing he—"

Gamadge suddenly put his hands on the arms of his chair and leaned forward as if he were going to rise. "Where is it?"

"Here, of course. You saw it." She lifted the silk bag from her arm and opened it. "Why?"

CHAPTER SIX

Peculiar Shade of Blue

GAMADGE SAID NOTHING, and Mrs. Coldfield took
the tightly bound paper book out of her bag, turned it upside
down, riffled the pages and shook it. She said: "Markers in it—
an old envelope and a piece of cellophane. The cellophane's
gone."

A bluish, square envelope fell out of the book; Gamadge
put out his hand for it, but the cat Junior was too quick for him.
Being a cat, he loved paper and had been brought up on paper
playthings. He sprang up, batted the envelope from Gamadge's
fingers, followed it to the floor and rolled on it.

Gamadge bent and snatched it up. He said: "Keep your
clumsy paws out of this, will you?" and flattened the square
of lilac-blue. He turned it over, looked at the sprawling but
impressive handwriting of the address, the postmark, the
pale old red stamp with the classical-looking woman's head,
crowned. He was motionless so long that Mrs. Coldfield
stopped playing with Junior to stare.

Gamadge said almost in a whisper: "cellophane."

"What on earth, Mr. Gamadge...?"

"You said there was a piece of cellophane."

"Yes, there was. What about the piece of cellophane?" She had begun to laugh, but stopped when she saw the absorbed look on his face.

He turned, and she thought how green his eyes were; she hadn't noticed before. "You never happened to look at this envelope, did you, Mrs. Coldfield?"

"Glen had a lot of correspondents. No, I don't think I—but I do remember that it was addressed to The Maples, and I'm almost sure it was addressed to him."

"It's addressed to a Coldfield. A Mrs. Deane Coldfield."

"Why, that's Grandmother Coldfield—Glen's grandmother! She died years ago—before the war."

"It has an English postmark—Shale, Somerset. And this is a Victorian stamp." Gamadge lifted the envelope to peer closer. "Postmark dated 1875."

"Oh yes, it must be one that Grandfather Coldfield wrote her on one of his trips. She usually went with him, but not always, and she religiously kept all his letters. There was a whole box of them up among her things in the attic." She added: "What's so interesting? Nothing about Grandfather Coldfield was interesting, I can assure you of that. His letters certainly can't have been. He was a byword in the family for dullness."

Gamadge said in a flat voice: "It's a nice paper—you never got it anywhere but in England. Thin but tough for foreign correspondence—what letter writers they all are! And that tint—I never saw it except on English paper: that pale blue with just a suspicion of lilac. Nothing feminine about it; it's not mauve or lavender."

Mrs. Coldfield couldn't help being amused. She leaned over to look. "I wonder why Glen was using it as a bookmark."

"Wasn't using it as a bookmark," said Gamadge dryly. "And he'd protected it with that piece of cellophane that got thrown away."

Somewhat startled at his words and tone, she did not reply. "Did your husband go through his grandmother's letters?" asked Gamadge. "I mean recently?"

"He and Ames looked them over after she died; they weren't even locked up, just in one of those little rosewood writing desks, as they call them; but I never saw what use such a desk could be."

"You mightn't find conveniences at the inn," said Gamadge. "I dare say that desk was older than Mrs. Deane Coldfield."

"I know she lived to a great age. Glen and Ames looked at some of the correspondence, but it was just too dull, so they left it."

"Up in the attic?"

"Yes," she said, more and more surprised. "They shoved all her things up there—it wasn't a good period, Grandmother Coldfield's heyday, but Ira never wants anything thrown away; or even sold. There are some pretty ornaments; I think they could be used, at any rate I'd use them. But not at The Maples as it is now—" she laughed—"straight McKinley."

Gamadge was turning the envelope gently with the edges of his fingers. Puzzled, she went on: "I saw those letters of Grandfather Coldfield's myself, once—we were poking around in the attic ages ago." Suddenly she paused and frowned. "You know—come to think of it, they were white."

Gamadge raised his eyes.

"White," she repeated, looking surprised. "White and shiny and bigger than that a little. Funny. I suppose Grandmother Coldfield had other correspondents in England."

Gamadge asked: "Where would you hide a letter?"

"I'm sure I don't know."

"Would it be a bad idea to hide it in another old letter?"

"Mr. Gamadge, what is that thing, and what are you talking about?"

"As a document man I should describe this thing as high explosive; as your private investigator, I should say it represents the motive we've been looking for."

She was astounded: "Motive for *murder*?"

"This envelope is evidence; if it had fingerprints on it, it constituted proof for your husband—proof of something he thought of as a crime." Gamadge looked at her and smiled. "He protected the prints with cellophane; but the cellophane is lost, and where is his proof now?"

"I shouldn't think there'd be much left of it," she answered in bewilderment.

"No, but it probably has your prints on it, and mine, and excellent ones of Junior's pads. I'll work on it tomorrow, anyway, and I'll take your prints before I do."

"But what is it evidence *of*?"

Gamadge was still too much fascinated by the blue envelope to answer her. He said: "You took it away with you in the crossword book, and after you were gone the murderer had a thorough search for it. There was a good chance that it had been thrown away. You knew nothing of it—your husband had promised not to tell anybody, to leave confession to the transgressor. When you came back and never spoke of it, the murderer was quite sure it had gone for good. Your life wasn't in danger, Mrs. Coldfield, after you came back from Dalgren's; it isn't now."

"Mr. Gamadge, won't you tell me what it's all about?"

"I'll do better than tell you; I'll show you in print."

He got up, went across the room to a shelf piled with magazines, and brought back a thick, buff-colored periodical, with a serious and responsible look about it. He sat down again and showed it to her. "You know this?"

"*The University Quarterly*? Oh yes, Ames takes it."

"Did your husband read it?"

"We both did."

"You know of course that it comes out, stubbornly attached as it is to its own ways, in February, May, August and November; my copy reaches me a few days before the first of the month. I dare say that you wouldn't have had a chance to look at the February number?"

"No, I haven't seen it."

"But your husband saw it. He died on the night of January the thirtieth—a Sunday. He may have seen this current copy of the *Quarterly* that very day. If he did, he came across this—the first article in the book, by Ranley, a top-flight critic. It's under their usual heading for the leading piece: LIFE AND LETTERS."

Frowning, she took the magazine from him. She read:

THE GARTHWAIN DISCOVERY

and looked up at Gamadge. "Does it mean Garthwain the poet?"

"That's who it means," said Gamadge. "The last of the great Victorians, and if he wasn't a Tennyson or a Browning or a Matthew Arnold he was certainly a runner-up, wasn't he? Morally he had them beat. Longer beard, too."

"Matthew Arnold didn't—"

"Only the whiskers. Don't think *I* don't love those three; more than I love Garthwain. It was a little late in the day for him to be so all-fired romantic."

"I used to be fond of Garthwain." She read on:

Garthwain's newly discovered *Letters to an Unknown* must rank as one of the great literary amazements of all time. They are not only fine examples of the poet's prose style, but they provide a mystery which...

Mrs. Coldfield laid the book down on the arm of her chair, gazed blankly at Gamadge, and said: "Mr. Gamadge, you can't mean that Mark Garthwain's *Letters to an Unknown* were written to *Grandmother Coldfield*?"

"I must beg you," said Gamadge earnestly, "to lower your voice a little. You and I are two of a very small number of persons now living who know the fact."

"Fact? How can you—"

"There's a facsimile of the great man's handwriting later on; take a look at it, and then at this envelope. His home was in Shale, Somerset. There's a description of the paper the letters were written on—that shape and size, and that peculiar shade of blue. There are eleven letters, no envelopes, and some of them are dated 1875. I'm used to handwriting—I only needed a look."

Mrs. Coldfield compared the facsimile and the writing on the envelope. "Good Heavens," she said faintly, "they *are* the same."

"Distinctive fist, isn't it?"

"Are they—are they love letters?"

"Mrs. Coldfield, they are compromising love letters. That's what provides the amazement. The old boy was at least fifty in those days, and his romance was all supposed to be in his poetry, for it wasn't in his life, so far as anybody knew. His marriage wasn't much of a romance, to hear his friends on the subject."

"Was he married—at the *time*?"

"Married and a monument. I won't say an institution," said Gamadge, "but certainly a monument."

Mrs. Coldfield leaned back in her chair. After a minute she sat forward again: "But couldn't he have written Grandmother Coldfield just one letter—about something else? Perhaps she was a literary admirer."

"If so he didn't keep her letter, which in that case was the only fan letter he never did keep. There were bales of them. And there's not a trace of her in his life. You know how the things are addressed? *To the Fairest*. What was Grandmother Coldfield like, when she was in her prime?"

"Perfectly beautiful," admitted Mrs. Coldfield, "but a little strange. Her portrait is in the dining-room; Grandfather Coldfield had it done in London."

"Ah! They met in the artist's studio. Perhaps at a garden party, though; Garthwain became quite a social character in his middle period. How old would she have been?"

"About thirty, I should think. She was fearfully old when she died—in 1935. Practically bedridden. We hardly saw her. Glen said they were all terrified of her, but that she had the reputation of being charming when she was young."

"Didn't wear well." Gamadge lifted the envelope carefully, studied it, and smiled at her. "You know what I think. She got these communications over a short period of time—a few years; she hid them in letters which she had received in the past from Grandfather Coldfield—nobody was likely to look into those! Ames and your husband looked at them, though, after her death—and your husband, or perhaps both of them, noticed some blue enclosures. Your husband paid no attention to them—why should he?

"But on the Sunday, the day he died—do you remember what he was doing that day, Mrs. Coldfield?"

"It was rainy, and he was in pain most of the time. He just wandered around the house, or read, or rested. I was out in the afternoon."

"Let's say he went up to the attic and tackled those old letters for want of something better to do. The blue enclosures were gone, all but one forgotten envelope. He'd read the article in the new *Quarterly*, he compared the handwriting, and he came to my conclusions. Did he have a fingerprinting outfit?"

"Yes, he did once, something he'd amused himself with when he was a boy."

"He wasn't amusing himself with it this time; somebody had cashed in on the Garthwain letters, and even if the envelopes had been withheld, it might only be a matter of time before they were cashed in on too. This *Quarterly* article is just a preview, you know, an introduction; the letters themselves are going to come out later, in a book; with a lot of commentary and so forth by George Files."

"Glendon got fingerprints on that envelope?" She sat staring at it.

"That's my idea; he'd only need powder and a good reading glass to satisfy himself—by comparison. Plenty of prints to be picked up around a house, you know, and plenty of them could be easily identified. When he had satisfied himself, he tackled the bandit—you said that would be his way of doing things."

"Yes."

"Serious matter, you know; somebody got a pretty penny out of it, and it wasn't the kind of thing the family would care for. So he showed his proof, and gave his ultimatum. But the guilty party didn't have to confess after all."

"No."

"All Grandmother Coldfield's fault, wasn't it?" asked Gamadge, with a change of tone. "She must have had an extraordinary kind of humor, mustn't she? And the sort of loving-kindness you meet in Restoration drama. Think of her laying this time-fuse to blow up her relatives-in-law with them. You know, I don't believe she can have liked the Coldfields."

"She had very little in common with them, I should say. She came of an old gone-to-seed family, and the impression I got was that she married almost frankly for a living. That's why the family didn't entirely like her. But she could be very charming, and usually was while she was young. Glendon had something of her charm, I understand, but he lacked her business instincts." She smiled. "Susan inherited her gracefulness." She looked up. "It's almost incredible—she must have known that her papers would be gone through after she died."

"But they weren't, after all—until that rainy Sunday, if I'm right. Still, she accepted the chance. I bet she was gloating. She didn't know what spectacular results her little practical joke would have, but I wonder if she'd have cared. I'm not surprised that she turned out rather formidable in her old age."

"But I don't understand how the letters could have been sold without giving anything away."

"Nothing's given away in this article," said Gamadge, "and I'm as curious about the circumstances of the sale as you are. More so, perhaps, since I know how those things are usually swung. It all happened in England; says here that they were offered to a well-known collector by an 'accredited agent'—

whatever that may mean. The collector couldn't bear to suppress anything so valuable—or perhaps he couldn't bear missing the spotlight—so he talked to Stanwood the publisher, and Stanwood took on the job of processing the Garthwain heirs. They're only collaterals, it's not even the same name, and it rather emerges that they need the money. They agreed to publication—sold the rights. Stanwood of course paid them. The implication is that Garthwain's Unknown has impecunious heirs too, and that they sold out under conditions of absolute secrecy."

"I should think so! The Coldfields would die first. But one of them *must* have—how frightful."

"Suppose it wasn't a born Coldfield, though?"

"Even so, I simply can't imagine…"

"There was certainly an agent," said Gamadge, "but how in that case was the deal swung? Well, I'll make inquiries in the trade. Those people sometimes know or guess more than gets into print. And now would you like to assess the money value of this envelope of ours?"

"If there were no envelopes, they must all have been very suspicious at first."

"It's all here, in the *Quarterly*. They put fifty-seven varieties of experts on the job; you know there are lots of other holograph letters of Garthwain's extant for comparison. He wrote thousands of letters: too many." Gamadge studied the blue envelope and smiled. "I wish I knew how they ever managed that affair; it can't have been too easy in those days."

"Well, Grandfather Coldfield did leave her in London sometimes when he had to go to France."

"One glorious summer, and then eleven letters to America. I suppose poor Garthwain thought she'd destroy his, and I bet the ones *he* destroyed weren't nearly so romantic. What was Mrs. Deane Coldfield's first name? Something fatal—Lorelei?"

"Serene."

"What? No! Wonderful. Serene, fatal and terrible."

"It was an old family name, I believe. You really must see the portrait; the bonnet, the bustle and the parasol. And that smile."

"You must see Garthwain's."

"Oh, I often have; Olympian."

"Have you ever seen his wife's? She had a bonnet, and a bustle, and a parasol too. But—it doesn't seem fair."

"I didn't think I should ever be laughing at all this."

"Best thing in the world for you, but we must get back to the grimmer side of it again before we drop it for tonight. Who among the Coldfields needed a substantial sum of money about a year ago? The deal was swung in England last March."

"I don't know. I do know that none of them went abroad."

"Remember that we've definitely decided on an agent. And what a trusted one! Who among the Coldfields may have needed money? You always look uncomfortable when you're deceiving me," said Gamadge. "I can find out by elimination. Ames? He's living on an annuity and they don't stretch. Not Ames, you think."

"Mr. Gamadge, how can I guess wildly?"

"Easy. Let's see—Ira isn't making too much money, and he's in a business where money is always welcome. Doesn't fill the bill? Too much family piety?"

"I can't imagine Ira—"

"Susan is marrying all kinds of money—"

"And they give her everything."

"Your sister-in-law; not a Coldfield, and she leads her own life. Can she do that on her housekeeping allowance? Ah, she's the one."

"It's only that she's always complaining about wanting more, but she wouldn't know anything about those letters. She hasn't the knowledge, or the interest—"

"Never underrate the frivolous. They can do things that would amaze you. Well, I'm inclined to agree with you—that's a dead end for the present. Now about the poisonings—and I may remark that it was splendid news for the poisoner, that you'd come home from Dalgren's to accuse someone unspecified of homicidal mania. You didn't know a thing. I bet the poisoner would have been glad to take your word and let you go, but couldn't step out of line to say so. About the poisonings: I suppose you've been over that ground again and again."

"Yes. Everything."

"So there's no means of knowing who dispensed amytal the first time? Or the night of the attempt on you?"

"No, none at all. I left Glen with his light on, in bed reading. The lemonade was in a glass on his bedside table, and anybody could have come in to say goodnight."

"And kindly put his capsule into the glass for him, and added the three others?"

"I suppose so."

"How about that soup of yours?"

"The kitchen-maid left the tray in the hall, and went back downstairs to get something she'd forgotten. She told me so. She isn't very good at trays, she only obliges on Agnes's day off."

"And that's a dead end too." He got up, locked the envelope in a file, and came back to hold out his hand. "Forget it till tomorrow."

She took his hand and let him help her to her feet. "Forget Mark Garthwain and Grandmother Coldfield?"

"You have my permission to think of them," said Gamadge, "and I shall probably meet them in my dreams. Aren't you feeling as I am—a little weighed down by this top secret? I am, I can tell you. Four people know it; you and I and the murderer, and the agent. That agent. Well, we'll leave him until tomorrow, but I wish I had information sufficient to allow me to get him out of bed."

"Wouldn't he be in England?"

"Oh no, he's an intimate trusted friend. He's here."

Junior, yawning and stretching, followed them out of the office. But he went into his act as soon as they reached the hall, and bounded in front of them up the stairs.

"He doesn't really like the elevator," said Gamadge. "He all but catches himself in the door. We let him think it's out of commission."

CHAPTER SEVEN

Inside Stuff

M ISS MULLINS THE NURSERY governess had had
too many employers—most of them fairly young people, of
course—to be surprised when she found Mrs. Gamadge and
guest in Miss Mullins's chintz-hung room on Friday morning,
letting down the hem of one of Mrs. Gamadge's dresses. She
wasn't surprised when Mrs. Gamadge casually told her that
Mrs. Coldfield's bags hadn't come. When Mr. Gamadge came
in and took Mrs. Coldfield's fingerprints, and then wiped her
fingers off with cleansing tissue and gasoline, Miss Mullins
didn't bat an eye.

Employers were so completely outside Miss Mullins's
restricted scheme of life that she never even tried to make
sense of them any more; it wasn't funnier for Mrs. Coldfield
to come to visit with nothing but a dinner dress, or for Mr.
Gamadge to take her fingerprints, than for other employers to
take ballet lessons (the husband, too) in their drawing-room, or
keep a masseur to operate on them (the wife, too) in the small

hours, or go to cold places for fun in winter, or give away their opera tickets and yet buy the tickets every year.

The Gamadges were very nice, and it didn't matter to Miss Mullins that they ate their meals wherever they happened to sit down, and had no dining-room, and treated their animals like people and treated people all alike. The little boy seemed normal.

She assured Mrs. Coldfield that she had a very comfortable cot in the nursery, and she helped with the letdown hem; pressed it with her electric iron.

"Those black suède pumps will do," said Mrs. Gamadge, "and you could wear my little black hat."

After a while Mr. Gamadge came back. He said: "Just as I thought. Junior might as well have taken a polishing-mitt to it."

"Don't put all the blame on him," protested Mrs. Coldfield. "I did my share. But you didn't—you never touched it except by the edges, even when it was on the floor."

"He's conditioned," said Mrs. Gamadge. "He can't pick up a piece of paper normally any more. He can hardly deal a pack of cards."

Miss Mullins hardly bothered to listen.

When she had gone out of the room, Clara said: "We're going out now to try hotels."

"I'm on my way too. Back for lunch? I'll need my client's assistance this afternoon."

"Take the car," said Clara. "We'll do better on foot."

Half an hour later Gamadge climbed the stairs to Hall's place of business. Albert rose to greet him, looking anxious.

"It's all right," Gamadge assured him. "No chance of any trouble now."

"That's good; but I think he's forgotten about it anyway."

Albert pushed open one of the folding-doors; J. Hall was having his elevenses, coffee and a bun; he looked around the back of his chair.

"This time," said Gamadge, "I only want some information."

"And why must I supply it?" asked Hall testily.

"Because you're in the book and manuscript trade, and you're an Englishman."

"I've only been naturalized forty years, that's so."

Gamadge laughed. He came and sat down on the leather chair opposite Hall, and lighted a cigarette. "I'm very much interested in the Garthwain discovery."

"Oh indeed?" Hall stared. "Only now? It's been no secret for months."

"You see? No secret to you, but I'm still gaping since I read Ranley's article in the *Quarterly*."

Hall leaned over to call to Albert. "Albert, Albert. What did I do with the new *University Quarterly*?"

Albert came in and found it in a tottering heap of pamphlets and catalogues. Then he went out, closed the doors behind him, and could be heard tapping faintly on a typewriter. He had recently persuaded Hall out of keeping him to longhand.

"Deal went through," said Hall, turning pages, "in March '48."

"I have a professional interest," said Gamadge, "in the way it was swung."

"So have a good many other people. I only know what I hear. I was over there last Spring myself." Suddenly Hall got out his large silk handkerchief, rubbed his nose with it, and began to laugh. The laugh was interrupted by deep bass chokings and coughings, from which he recovered sufficiently to get out some words: "Can't help it. Poor Garthwain. Poor Wordsworth, Dickens, Ruskin, and now poor old Garthwain."

"The others have survived," said Gamadge severely. "I suppose Garthwain will."

"Who ever said you were a moralist, my boy? It's shockin'."

"Just forget morals and tell me how on earth that deal went through. What do they mean—'accredited agent'?"

"Funny, isn't it? Well, the agent was a solicitor."

"No!"

"Smart work, wasn't it? Nobody can make him say a thing, and Doddington wouldn't anyway. You know Doddingtons'?"

Gamadge shook his head.

"Very old-established firm, Doddingtons'. Generations of 'em. He simply offered the letters at face value: are they authentic? And if they are, will you meet the price? He took 'em to Locker."

"Oh, that was the collector, was it?"

"That was the feller, and he has plenty of money to buy anything that takes his fancy. He had everything done to those letters, he put all the new scientific fellers on to them. They're Garthwain letters, no doubt of it."

"I'm sure they are."

"And of course the theory is that they were brought to Doddington in secrecy by the Unknown's heirs, who reserved the envelopes from reasons of delicacy. They'll dig it out yet, they'll dig it out."

"Perhaps."

"But not through Doddingtons'. Well, of course Locker pretended to hang back a little—no envelopes, no guarantee that there wouldn't be trouble about them later. But then Doddington gave his own guarantee—money back if there *was* trouble—and the price was reasonable. About ten thousand, it would come to, with Doddingtons' commission deducted. Locker bought 'em, of course."

"Any hitch with the Garthwain heirs about publication?"

"Well, no; like a lot of geniuses, Garthwain didn't have much talent to spare for his family. They're a dull lot, I understood, but Stanwood had to pay them for publication rights—a good fat sum. I didn't hear how much."

"Stanwood will get it back."

"And a little over. A little over. Who's going to do the book? I forget."

"Files."

"That's it, and it will be translated into—" Hall began to choke again. "You know, Gamadge, I wouldn't be surprised if it got on the films."

Gamadge smoked in silence while Hall enjoyed himself. At last he said: "I'd like your opinion about something."

"Have it, my dear boy, for what it's worth."

"We both know what it's worth in these matters. The thing's very interesting; mystery and all. May I put a hypothetical question?"

"What is it?"

"Well, suppose the owners of the letters are shyer than we think. Too shy to appear in the transaction at all. I mean, they might feel that they were selling out—old-fashioned way of putting it—the family honor."

"They were," said Hall, looking surprised.

"Well, they'd be very shy. Suppose they confided the business to an agent?"

"Eh?"

"A confidential agent. Suppose he went to Doddington?"

Hall gazed at him over the silk handkerchief.

"With the guarantee," continued Gamadge, "and the explanation that his principals couldn't in decency appear. You know what Doddington is like; would he deal?"

"Would he deal without knowing the provenance of the letters?" Hall thought it over. "If he knew the agent personally, say as a client of the firm—"

"And knew he was good for ten thousand dollars and Doddingtons' fee," Gamadge put in.

"It wouldn't be only a question of the money, you know that," said Hall. "Doddingtons' wouldn't risk their reputation; very bad for the firm if the letters turned out to be stolen property. Yes, they'd have to know that agent pretty well—well enough to accept his word."

"It would be a take it or leave it proposition," said Gamadge. "And the agent's name would have to be kept as secret as though it were the principal's."

"If it provided a clue to the principal, yes."

"Even nationality might provide a clue," said Gamadge, smiling, "with the whole literary world turned detective."

Hall cocked an eye at him.

"Say he was a Scot," suggested Gamadge. "Or an Irishman. That might narrow things down."

"It might. Well," said Hall, "if I had confidence in the agent, I'd go ahead myself."

"That's enough for me." Gamadge pulled himself up out of the chair.

"Why are you so sure there was an agent?" asked Hall, watching him.

"Those delicate-minded owners. In their place I should have used an agent, but I'd have picked him with care. I suppose there simply wasn't any way for them to sell the envelopes too, and yet protect themselves. They'd have got twice the money."

"It's tantalizing," agreed Hall. "Well, we can't help it—we all turn scavenger in the end. Why don't you devote the rest of your life to finding those envelopes, Gamadge? Nice hobby."

"I will, if you'll devote the rest of yours to finding Tome 1 of that Molière I got off you. It must be somewhere, which is more than we can assume of the Garthwain envelopes."

"Oh, nobody in their senses would destroy the Garthwain envelopes," protested Hall. "If those delicate-minded owners ever got hungry enough, they'd sell. Why, they're insurance. Absolutely safe bet—they'd match up with every date on every letter."

Gamadge laughed and took his leave.

When he reached home he found that Mrs. Coldfield had quarters at a quiet midtown hotel, and that Clara had placed a couple of bags at her disposal in case her luggage wasn't forthcoming at The Maples.

"I only hope you'll get safely away from the place yourself," she told him, half in earnest. "I have such a horror of it now, I'm almost afraid to let you go there."

"They'll give me anything I want, just to get rid of me."

"Perhaps you'd better take dear Mr. Bantz along with you."

"I won't need him this time."

"And it's going to rain like anything."

"And there's no porte-cochère."

"Harold could hold your umbrella for you," said Clara.

They had lunch, and after they had finished their coffee Gamadge took Mrs. Coldfield down to the office and installed her at his desk beside the windows.

"Here are pencils," he said, "and here's paper, and you'll find the telephone book and other reference books on that revolving stand there." He pulled up a chair beside her. "I've been making inquiries about the sale of the letters, and I'm afraid we can't hope for the name of that agent—not unless we show cause to enlist the services of Scotland Yard. Or the Home Secretary? Lord Chancellor? Who is it in England that can make a solicitor give a client away?"

"Was it done through a solicitor?"

"Yes; he got a guarantee of refund if the letters turned out to be stolen goods, but he got even more. He got an impression of bona fides; that means he knows the agent of old. And it means something more to me; if the agent was as responsible as all that, he wouldn't take a chance either. He's sure, absolutely sure there'll be no trouble about the theft of those letters, even if it's discovered by the Coldfields." Gamadge looked at her, quietly smoking. "He was sure at the time, and he's sure now."

"Because a Coldfield took them, and he knows there would never be any scandal allowed in that family?"

"Yes; the whole thing would be suppressed; they'd keep it to themselves, and take their medicine. They might turn out the black sheep, but nobody would ever know why. The agent knows them pretty well, Mrs. Coldfield."

She nodded, pencil in hand, her eyes on his.

"And of course it's very improbable that the agent knows anything about the real consequences of the theft," continued Gamadge. "He probably doesn't even guess. He knows the thief well, but not well enough to be told that. So all he's done has been to receive stolen goods, perhaps partly owned by the thief anyway, and which so far as he and the thief knew were a treasure trove. The Coldfields didn't know they had them, and weren't being cheated of money because they'd never have cashed in on them."

"Would the agent think of all that as an *excuse*?"

"He would certainly try. He seems to be a man of reputation, if he is a man, and he seems to have acted out of friendship. Fifty per cent of the net wouldn't be excessive as commission in such a case; would five thousand dollars pay him, or the thief either, for this job?"

"Did they—did those letters really bring ten thousand dollars?"

"There's a lot more than literary value in them, you know; there's news value and shock value. Everybody concerned will get big advertising, everybody except the people that don't want it. Now what I want, of course, is a list of people, friends of the Coldfields, who can or may fill our requirements. It's not so difficult as it looks—no need for discouragement." Gamadge smiled at her.

"Well, at least we know that he was over in England to make the sale."

"Over in England, somewhere about March of last year—not later than March, so I'm told. You can therefore eliminate very old people, very sick people, very young people, people who wouldn't be taken seriously as intermediaries in such a deal. The agent wasn't a mere business acquaintance of any Coldfield—he knew them at home. He was somebody's friend."

"Susie's friends are all young; and none of them would do."

"I don't suppose they would. And don't forget that the agent had to give Doddington a ten thousand dollar guarantee. Watch the credit rating!"

"Mr. Gamadge—" she dropped her pencil, it rolled, and Gamadge caught it before it fell to the floor. "Mr. Gamadge, it simply isn't possible to be fair about this. You have to use psychology."

"That's fair," said Gamadge, amused.

"I mean Ira's cronies—there isn't one of them that couldn't and wouldn't lend him ten thousand dollars outright, rather than—"

"Mrs. Coldfield, if you were hard up enough to need ten thousand dollars as badly as this party needed it, would you feel particularly anxious to pay it back again?"

"I'll have to think of somebody they *all* know."

"You've thought already."

"I'm going to be fair."

"That's right."

"No psychology. I'm going to put them all down—all I can't eliminate."

"Just eliminate Ira Coldfield's stock exchange buddies, will you? Friendship is friendship, but sense is sense. And you might eliminate the Watertons."

She couldn't help laughing.

By the time Mrs. Coldfield had finished her list, and Gamadge had studied it, and they had all had tea, the rain was coming down in buckets. There was wind, too—half a gale.

"Lovely afternoon for a drive up the river," said Clara.

"Just slow driving, that's all." Gamadge had turned on the radio. "They say the wind's going down, and it's going to clear later."

"I feel guiltier than ever," said Mrs. Coldfield. "I do wish you'd put it off."

"Put it off? I can't wait to get there. I'm particularly anxious to meet the family doctor."

"I never liked him, but his grandchildren are rather nice. They're friends of Susie's, always in and out of the house. Or were." She wrinkled her forehead. "I haven't seen much of them this year. But I suppose they're busy. The boy is a medical student, and I think the girl has some job too."

"Don't you know their parents?"

"Oh, they're orphans. They live with their grandfather in the village. They were really all brought up together—the Smyth children, and Susie, and Jim Waterton."

CHAPTER EIGHT

Miracle

SOON AFTER FIVE O'CLOCK the wind dropped, and the storm subsided to a thin, steady fall of rain. Gamadge was able to make pretty good speed after all.

Whenever he had to stop, he snatched a typewritten sheaf of notes out of his pocket and studied them. They were his digest of Sylvia Coldfield's list; he had made some eliminations of his own, and the list now read:

Salmon, A. T.
Funny old character, seems old at sixty odd. Retired. Was in the automobile business, and seems to have a modest competence. Bachelor, lives in hotels. Is devoted to the Coldfields, says they are the only family he has. Goes there regularly to stay. Knew them well as a neighbor when they had a house in New York. Hobby, rare books and prints. Travels a great deal, and was abroad last year. Epicure and gourmet.

Barrette, Myra.
Spinster, about fifty years old, contemporary of Ames
Coldfield. Lives in a medium-priced apartment hotel
in New York, travels a great deal, was in Europe last
Spring. Once had more money, kept a flat in London.
Is a close family friend; brought up with Ames and Ira,
part of their childhood circle in New York. Is very fond
also of Mrs. Ira Coldfield, who enjoys her company and
always welcomes her at The Maples. Hobby, bridge
and backgammon. Was in England for months every
year until the war. Is said to have knocked around a
little when younger, had a lot of amusing gossip, and a
very frivolous? tough? attitude towards life.

Venner, William Cole.
Son of Venner the famous antique dealer and appraiser.
Carries on the business wholesale, and his business
seems to be his hobby. Perhaps forty years old, good-
looking, pleasant, travels regularly abroad. Met the
Coldfields when they were getting rid of their house
and furniture in New York some years ago, and is on
very friendly terms with them now. Drops in on his
business trips around the country, comes up for dinner.
Bachelor, so far as Sylvia Coldfield knows. She never
heard him speak of any relatives.

Holls, Gregory.
Classmate of Ira Coldfield's. Sporting character,
retired from practice of the law. Plays golf with Ira,
goes fishing with him, often stays the week end at The
Maples. Wife dead, and he lives at his club. Ira's father
is supposed to have given him a helping hand when
he left college and started in law practice. A colorless
type of man, but fits in. Was on a long cruise last year,
visited a lot of places, ended up in England and came
back here in May.

Gamadge had his last look at the list when he slowed up at the Coldfield gates. He sat looking out at the house and grounds before he turned in; in this rainy light the place was bleak enough, but it could never be very gay. There were a lot of the big old trees, which matched the color of the rough stone building and stables; and the ugly stone seemed to soak up the rain.

But that house wouldn't be damp inside; it had been built as tight as a drum, built for permanence and comfort, and its woodwork would be as good as new. Certainly the big sunken door was; Gamadge, surveying it grimly, wondered how he and Harold could ever have got anybody out of the place.

He tried to draw upon his historical sense, but he simply couldn't imagine those square blue envelopes coming to that door; or did Mrs. Deane Coldfield have to drive down to the post office herself, in the shining carriage or—more probably— in her neat dog-cart, to get her foreign mail? But she could always explain that her English correspondent was a lady, that dear kind Lady Totten, who hadn't much of interest to say.

Gamadge roused himself from this reverie and rolled the car down over fine wet gravel to the doorstep. A plump maid let him in, took his card, and ushered him into the drawing-room on the left of the hall. She lighted lamps, and went away.

There were closed folding-doors at the end of the room, shutting it off from the library of Harold's description. Gamadge stood and looked around him. A fine well-proportioned parlor, but it would have looked better with the original fringed and looped curtains at the high windows, the original fringed and buttoned furniture and the crystal chandelier. It had been done over at the turn of the century, and Gamadge felt hemmed in by the gimcrack gilt and the brown velvet and the tapestry that now bore witness to the Coldfield lack of taste. He was sure that Mrs. Deane Coldfield hadn't cared for this; but when it was done she was perhaps fifty-five years old, already a dowager.

This generation of Coldfields took its time; the family was evidently studying his card. After something of a wait the folding-doors were pushed open, and a small, slender, greying man stood between them. He said: "Mr. Gamadge: do come in."

Gamadge advanced into a handsome library; there were plenty of books in glassed cases, there was a fire burning in a wide hearth, there were comfortable chairs and sofas and a carved oak table. A man and two women sat in the chairs that faced him as he came in; the man rose—a tall, big, ruddy man: Ira Coldfield.

Ames was pale, with pale blue eyes. He held out his hand. "Mr. Gamadge," he said in his high, carefully accented voice, "I find I know you by reputation. Your books. We are all so much interested. We had no idea." He looked greatly amused.

Gamadge shook hands and said he was gratified.

"Since I do know you, after a fashion," continued Ames, "I'd better introduce you and the family. I myself am Ames Coldfield. That is my sister-in-law Georgette, and the young woman is my niece Susan. And there, scowling at you, though he knows better than to do it, is my brother Ira."

Gamadge nodded amiably to the others. Mrs. Ira bowed in a formal way, Susan smiled faintly at him, Ira's face did not change.

"Had we but known!" said Ames with his giggle. "And had you but known that your name was a passport into this house at any time."

"That wasn't exactly the idea." Gamadge, now completing the wide circle in front of the fire, with the others opposite him and Ames on his left, had the big oak table on his right. He leaned against a corner of it, and spoke amiably. "The idea was to get Mrs. Glendon Coldfield out, passport or no passport."

"And you succeeded," chuckled Ames, "in the most romantic way. It was comical, too, from one point of view. Mine, in fact; I saw the strategy from the dining-room, and the departure when I got out on the doorstep. Adventure in the home. I haven't been so stimulated since my Anthony Hope days. I can read him yet."

Gamadge wasn't paying much attention to this highly civilized approach. He let his eyes wander over the others—Ira Coldfield, with his clipped blond moustache and his angry blue eyes; Mrs. Ira, handsome in her red dress and her gold jewelry. She had hazel eyes, bright bronze hair, plenty of make-up, a good figure verging on heaviness, a hard stare. The hazel eyes were a little prominent, and they looked frightened.

Susan Coldfield had the hazel eyes, and the bronze hair—but it was the bronze that her mother's had been long ago. Her coloring was natural and beautiful, her features fine, her bones smaller than Georgette Coldfield's. She was in a dark-green dress, very smart and plain. Her expression was one of mortification.

Ira put a stop to his brother's speech. He said furiously: "There's no occasion for all this."

"None," agreed Gamadge. "You can't want me in the house longer than necessary. I shall deliver your sister-in-law's message, collect her luggage, and go."

Ira said loudly: "I don't want to hear her message—I know well enough what it will be. I tell you and I tell her that I don't give an inch, and neither does my wife or my brother. She was in a crazy, dangerous state of mind, and we shouldn't have been safe in the house with her if she hadn't been restrained—in the most humane, kindest way. Ask her doctor."

"I should like to," said Gamadge. "I was looking forward to it. But I don't see him."

There was a short pause. Then Ira burst out: "He was to be here."

"But he drove out of town," said Susan dryly. "Very important call, you know."

Her mother turned on her sharply: "Susan, this affects you. That's why you're here now. Please remember it."

Gamadge said equably: "Let me deliver the message; it will make a difference in your point of view. Mrs. Glendon Coldfield withdraws her statement."

The pause was longer this time; even Susan looked stupefied. Ames put his hand up to *his* little clipped moustache, Ira stood as if frozen to the carpet, his wife, her eyes on Gamadge, swallowed hard on nothing.

At last Ames spoke—tentatively. "You mean she now says she was mistaken?"

"Quite mistaken," replied Gamadge. "Nobody went mad and poisoned her husband, nobody went mad and tried to poison her. She sees that clearly."

Ames said after a moment: "But this is a miracle. I assure you, Mr. Gamadge—but you can't know, of course, what she's put us through. Not in detail."

Ira asked in a flat voice: "What made her change her mind?"

"Well, I may say I argued her out of the idea," said Gamadge.

Another pause, but nobody asked the obvious question. Susan, looking triumphant, was smiling; perhaps the answer to the question was so clear to all but one of them that there was no reason to ask it. One of them would never ask it.

"In that case," said Ames, astonishment giving way to what certainly resembled relief, "let's all sit down. You must hear our side of it, Mr. Gamadge—you really must. You've earned our eternal gratitude, we now regard you as our dearest friend. A miracle!" He looked at the others. "How shall we reward him?"

"We might ask him," said Susan dryly, "what Sylvia would like."

"Oh—well, Mrs. Coldfield did suggest an adjustment," said Gamadge, taking the chair Ames pushed towards him. Ira slowly sank down on the one he had risen from when Gamadge came in, and Ames settled himself beside the fire. Mrs. Ira got a cigarette out of a gold box and nervously held it for her husband to light. She said: "I don't know what you mean—

adjustment. Surely she hasn't the nerve to expect *damages*, or something?"

Susan said: "Oh Mother," and turned her head away.

"Don't let such words sully the air," begged Ames, laughing, but Gamadge wasn't laughing. He said: "She's quite safe now, of course, and with friends who can protect her physically; but she'd like an assurance that insanity won't at any time in the future be imputed to *her*."

"We deserve that," said Susan.

"But why on earth," asked Mrs. Ira pettishly, "should there be any question of such a thing now, since she's come to her senses?'"

"Or at least we hope so," grumbled Ira. "We hope there'll be no relapse."

"Oh stuff and nonsense," said Ames. "Sylvia was in a wrought-up state, that's all. And in any case, she's out of our hands." He smiled at Gamadge. "Don't say thanks to you! Really we're not so formidable." He glanced up at a side door which evidently led into the back hall. "Yes? Who's that? Come in, come in. Oh, Miss Beal."

"She isn't wanted now," said Ira hurriedly.

But Miss Beal had come in and stood planted, her short, thick, muscular figure encased in its nursing whites, a sweater over her shoulders. She fixed alert eyes on Gamadge.

"This is Sylvia's nurse, Mr. Gamadge," said Ames, rising to smile at her. "Doctor Smyth's representative, since he couldn't come himself."

Ira said with some annoyance: "It's not necessary. Mrs. Glendon has withdrawn her statements, Miss Beal. Apparently she's responsible again. That's all."

Miss Beal, looking squarely at Gamadge, said sharply: "It isn't all. I want you to know I never thought she was crazy, and I never knew what statements she'd made. These people wouldn't believe it, but she didn't talk. I say she never would have talked. But it wasn't my business—I was paid to take care of her and keep her from annoying people writing letters and on the telephone, and a nurse does what the doctor says. If she don't, she's blacklisted with the agencies and the hospitals."

Ames said sweetly: "This comes a little late, Miss Beal, but we're delighted to hear it. And no blame attaches to you, I'm sure, in this gentleman's mind. But I must remind you that your patient"—he glanced smiling at Gamadge—"must have sent out at least one message."

"She certainly did not," said Miss Beal. "Somebody in the family must have talked, that's all." But her eyes were still on Gamadge's, and he thought they held appeal.

He said blandly: "The secrets of the prison-house will remain secrets between Mrs. Glendon Coldfield and myself."

Susan said wearily: "I wish we could stop this. I feel like one of those hideous people that ran the concentration camps."

"You needn't," snapped her mother. "For all the help you ever were…" She turned to Miss Beal. "All right, nurse," she said. "We shan't complain of you, and you won't talk about us; Mrs. Glendon Coldfield was Doctor Smyth's patient, and you seem to know already that there's professional etiquette involved. You can go home as soon as you pack."

"I am packed," said Miss Beal, "and I packed up for my patient, too. Her bags are ready; I put her summer things in her trunk. I'm glad she's getting a change. This case was on my nerves."

She walked out, closing the door smartly behind her.

Mrs. Coldfield sat looking at the closed door and smoking. She said: "I detest that woman."

"My dear," said Ames, "she's Smyth's responsibility, and I must say I think it was very feeble of him not to be here at any cost to talk to Mr. Gamadge."

"He didn't know," remarked Susan in her clipped young voice, "that Mr. Gamadge would be so polite."

Mrs. Ira turned to Gamadge, and asked: "Won't you smoke? There are cigarettes on the table beside you."

"Thank you." Gamadge got out his own and lighted one. Ames and Ira lighted cigarettes too, and they all relaxed a little. It was raining hard again—driving against the long windows, streaming down. Ames got up and drew the curtains.

Mrs. Coldfield said: "Mr. Gamadge, I'd like you to understand. Sylvia takes it back; but she wouldn't before, and how could we believe that she wasn't going to talk? She's talked to you."

"Quite different," said Gamadge. "You hadn't accepted her terms."

"Terms?"

"You kept her here as a prisoner."

"Mr. Gamadge," she said, her handsome face a mask of rage, "do you realize that she might have ruined Susan's life and disgraced us all?"

"We were trying," said Ames, "to keep a colossal scandal in the family. We adopted strong measures, yes, but I ask you—what could we have done? Call in Dalgren, let *him* have the story? Our own man, Smyth—he's a G.P., but a good man—thought she ought to be put away until she came to her senses—literally. You know yourself that doctors disagree. Smyth thought she was deteriorating, dangerous to herself. Damn it, we were at our wits' end."

Susan's voice cut sharply across these plaintive words: "Don't include me, Uncle Ames. I wanted to tell Jimmie all about it—he'd merely have laughed."

"The young," murmured Ames, "have a solution to everything."

"They don't know everything." Georgette Coldfield's face, turned away from her daughter's now, was a study in exasperation. "They don't know anything. No experience, no judgment, nothing but a lot of Old School sentiment. 'Jimmie wouldn't think this, Jimmie would think that.' Jimmie has parents," she finished, looking back at Susan with a threatening smile, "and they're thinking of their grandchildren already. They've talked enough about all those future splendid trusts. Are *you* crazy?"

"I don't think Sylvia was, just because she forgot she'd taken those capsules."

So here was somebody stepping up to the danger line as if it wasn't even there! At last! And, by Jove, thought Gamadge, stepping over it. "Mr. Gamadge," asked Susan, "how did you ever persuade Sylvia to remember?"

Through the stillness in the room Gamadge could hear the rain against the windows—even through the thick glass and the drawn velvet of the curtains. He put out his cigarette. "Well, I didn't," he said, "I just persuaded her that it's a very unusual thing—that sort of mania breaking out in a family without any premonitory signals, and nothing whatever in past history to account for it."

This line of discussion was broken by Ira Coldfield. He suddenly clapped his hands on his knees, got up as if he had come to a decision, and walked over to the fireplace. He put his hand on the mantel shelf, stood for a moment looking down into the flames, and then turned and faced Gamadge as man to man. "Mr. Gamadge," he said, "I feel that on the whole we've been very fortunate."

Gamadge looked inquiring.

"You put an end to an impossible situation," Ira went on in a friendly tone. "If your methods were unorthodox—"

"They had to be," said Gamadge cheerfully, "to match yours."

"I know, I know," said Ira, "it looks brutal now. But how do you think *we* felt—while it was going on? It wore us all down. If Sylvia was a prisoner, so were we—terrible state of anxiety."

"But was it comparable to hers?"

"She might have known us well enough to know that nothing very terrible was impending. After all she only suspected one of us of being a lunatic. You're welcome to hear exactly what we were arranging, and I may assure you that everybody was kind and friendly to her—Smyth was most kind. He couldn't be anything else. She was being treated as a mentally sick person, you know—psychotic."

"Mr. Coldfield," asked Gamadge gently, "have *you* ever been subject to physical coercion?"

"She had only to withdraw her statement, and she has withdrawn it."

Gamadge looked at him quietly, then he turned to look at the others. His eyes remained on Mrs. Coldfield.

"She was told," he said, "that it was too late to withdraw her statement."

"Mr. Gamadge," said Ira, "could we have believed after her original obstinate behavior about it that she meant what she said? Just try to believe me now, and assume that we were all acting in good faith."

"Glad to assume it," said Gamadge, "for the sake of argument."

"Well, you ought to know what we were trying to do about my sister-in-law. There's a non-judicial procedure in these cases, as Smyth found out for us; and it's a good thing, too—saves the patient embarrassment and distress of mind. No going into court, no publicity."

"Nicer for the relatives, too," said Gamadge.

"Yes," agreed Ira shortly, "nicer for the relatives—for everybody concerned. By that procedure, which is absolutely legal, a patient can be committed on petition of a relative or friend, and the certificate of one reputable physician. But—here's the hitch, if the relative wasn't acting in good faith—committed for only thirty days."

Gamadge said: "That's a good law. Of course a period of thirty days in some kinds of proprietary hospital might settle the question of the patient's sanity for all time." He added: "But I was to assume that you were acting in good faith."

"And so was Smyth," said Ira violently. "He was looking into the whole thing most carefully; I should have gone to the place myself. All we wanted—"

"I know."

"You might tell Sylvia. No use talking to her here—she wouldn't even listen."

"She didn't dare listen. She was bending all her faculties to the job of keeping calm. Try it sometime, Mr. Coldfield—try living in those conditions, with a nurse watching to see whether you won't show even normal reactions to them."

"But you won't look at our point of view."

"I'm looking at it. The situation was tough all round." He rose, and looked at Mrs. Coldfield. "I'd better be getting back to New York—if I might have that luggage to put in the car?"

She had been watching him narrowly during the last few minutes. Now, her face cleared of everything but polite concern, she got up too. "Mr. Gamadge, it's pouring; there'll be floods along the line. Won't you at least have your dinner before you go?"

Ames chimed in delightedly: "Georgy, I was hoping you'd suggest it! Gamadge, we won't take no for an answer."

"And you'll meet my young man," said Susan.

Ira said: "Hope you can manage it. And by the way, I meant to explain—as Sylvia knows, Ames and I are Glendon's executors. She inherits everything; I'm afraid it's not much. If she doesn't care to meet us, you could send along that lawyer to meet ours."

"I'll do that," said Gamadge. "Thanks for mentioning it. Our man is Robert Macloud."

"Ours is Dunham. Well, that's settled, and you're having dinner." Ira seemed relieved and cheerful now. "There's a good half hour yet, isn't there, Georgy?"

"Oh, more," said Mrs. Coldfield.

"Cloakroom downstairs, everything you need," said Ames, bustling forward. "Come in afterwards for a drink—my little study back here; I'm really looking forward very much to a talk with a first-class writing man."

"If I might telephone?"

"That's out here too," said Susan. "I'll show you."

(HAPTER NINE

Frustrated

THE SIDE DOOR OF THE LIBRARY came out towards the rear of the hall; there was a telephone stand under the stairs to the right, and to the left a dressing-room had been built in and panelled to match the older woodwork. It cut the hall in half lengthwise, and extended to the partition that contained the baize door of last night's adventure.

"You'll find it all rather out of date in there," said Susan, indicating the door of the dressing-room, "but quite complete."

"Modern improvement, wasn't it?"

"Yes, it was put in when they spoiled the rest of the house."

She smiled up at Gamadge, and he returned the smile. About twenty-five, full of life, delightful to look at she was. He sat down at the telephone. She was turning to go away, but he said: "Don't go. I'll only be a minute, but I mustn't keep the lady in suspense."

Half amused, half disturbed, she asked: "Did Sylvia think something awful would happen to you?"

"She didn't quite know what to think."

"I don't blame her." Susan frowned. "I may not sound very loyal to the family, but in her place—"

"You'd never be in her place, Miss Coldfield."

"Not enough character?" She smiled again.

"Plenty of character, not her kind."

He dialled the operator, got his home number, and spoke: "Clara? Hello. I'm up at The Maples, Cliffside you know, and they've been kind enough to invite me to stay for dinner. As it's such a rotten night, I've taken them up on it... Back early, though, rain or not... Yes, I'm bringing the bags... Goodbye."

He replaced the telephone and got up. Susan said: "Your voice was quite different. Of course you'd be married."

"Why not?"

"All the nicest are married, and it makes them a little dull."

"Isn't Mr. Waterton nice? And will marrying you make him dull?"

"He's a little dull already." She laughed. "It's part of his charm. It's the way I like him."

"You're in love with that character," said Gamadge, studying her. "Crazy about him."

"So I am. Mr. Gamadge, Sylvia never said anything about you or your wife—being her friends."

"Miss Coldfield, there are many pleasant things about you, and one of the things I find most encouraging is that you ask questions. Do you realize that you're the only member of your family that asks questions?"

"They're afraid to—you scare them. Mr. Gamadge, do try to remember that they're principally scared on my account."

"Your uncle Ames too?"

"With Uncle Ames it's family, all family. Oh, you should have been in the library when Agnes brought your card in; I was nervous too, of course, I thought you might turn out to be a detective with his hat on, and a cigar. But when Uncle read that card—he leaned over and hissed at us. 'Man's entirely respectable—he's a writer. This makes it different. Be civil, now.' All like that," said Susan, laughing heartily.

"I have my reward," said Gamadge. "Sometimes I thought I never would have it, but here it comes. Does being a writer make it all right to come in by the back door and deceive the cook? By the way, I'm sorry about that. I wish you'd tell her sometime that it's the only thing I do regret."

"I'll tell her, but she still thinks you're a nice gentleman. You know how they are—'Some mistake; he was a nice gentleman.'"

"Tell her I *am* a nice gentleman."

"She'll soon know all about it. I'll tell them all myself. How relieved they'll be; they hated Sylvia being out of her head and shut up with that horrible nurse. Now I can tell them it all *was* a mistake—for once."

"Good. Look here—I hope this isn't a dinner party? I wore old stout tweeds—afraid I might have to fight my way out of here, you know, maybe drop from a window."

"We won't dress."

"Go ahead and put on whatever you were going to wear for that young man."

"He won't dress either; he's bringing—"

A deep-toned bell pealed. Gamadge, pausing with his hand on the dressing-room door, watched her rush up the hall, swing the front door open, and throw her arms around the neck of a blond youth in a dripping raincoat. Behind him a slim girl in a hooded mackintosh called out: "Hey, let me in out of this rain," and ducked past him.

When Gamadge came out into the hall again he heard young voices and a shaking of ice in the drawing-room; he returned to the library by the side door, went back into the study, and found Ames there pouring cocktails carefully.

"Come in," said Ames, looking up at him. "My special brew, too good for untutored palates. I thought you might be willing to spare a frustrated man of letters a few minutes for a chat. Do sit down, Mr. Gamadge. You'll find cigarettes there beside you, and these hors d'oeuvres look appetizing."

Gamadge sat down, took his glass, sipped from it, and leaned back in his shabby, high-backed old stuffed chair. He was astonished to find that it was a patent rocker, the first he had seen since his grandmother's had been carted off to the village sale long ago.

The little den was as shabby, comfortable and out of date. He and Ames sat before a narrow grate built for coal, in which briquettes smouldered and glowed cozily. There were dried grasses in fan-shaped vases on the chimney piece, and between them an ancient night-clock.

"It doesn't work," said Ames, following Gamadge's eyes to the white globe with its circle of hours. "Not much of an ornament, either, but I like to keep it there. Reminds me a little of myself."

Gamadge looked at him, smiling. Ames might once have been a chubby man, but the fat had gone and left a certain flabbiness in his face and figure. He went on: "The fringes, the fringes."

Gamadge raised his eyebrows inquiringly.

"Of literature," said Ames with a sigh. "That's where I cling. Criticism of other people's criticism, comments on commentaries, letters in contributors' columns about this and that, little pieces—squibs—even parodies. All in good fun, you know, how could anybody object? More than willing to wound, but mortally afraid to strike."

Gamadge went on smiling.

"I wouldn't have rated mention in one of the Epistles, though," continued Ames. "But Mr. Pope would have made mincemeat of me in a different context. Ah well, there's more than one kind of immortality, but no great man would bother to transfix me nowadays."

All this was said with a kind of modest self-satisfaction. Gamadge had met the same kind of thing before, and had never been able to analyze it completely; it couldn't be just a simple pride in having failed to meet the standards of the market-place. He said: "There's decorative value in fringes; as a matter of fact I'm there myself."

"You? My dear Mr. Gamadge, you couldn't write a thing without producing a work of creation. Excuse the jargon, there are words one has to use or go dumb."

"Well, thanks," said Gamadge; "but I never aspired to anything higher than craftsmanship." He put out an arm and picked the current number of *The University Quarterly* from a pile of magazines on the table near him. Opening it at the Garthwain article, he showed the page to Ames Coldfield. "There's a certain comfort in obscurity, isn't there?"

Ames bent to look, laughed, and sat back again. "Incredible, isn't it? Poor old codger, what a flight to take in his years of discretion! The initiative, the peril!"

"And the emotion."

"And the emotion. And if we but knew it, the Unknown was a dumpy little tradesman's wife, golden-haired and with those large blue eyes that pop at you. I have second sight in these matters. She may even have been the landlady's daughter, and her parents stored up those Garthwain letters for future reference. And why did I use the word incredible?"

"I don't know," said Gamadge, laughing. "There have been precedents."

"Life and Letters," mused Ames. "Life and Letters—they are bracketed together for no bad reason. But I don't *think* we write quite so many letters in these days."

Gamadge, idly turning pages, suggested: "I shouldn't think the landlady's daughter's heirs would be so shy of disclosing themselves."

"Now my dear man!" protested Ames. "The respectable middle class! Do anything for money, but do it with decent subterfuge."

"Garthwain was no Bohemian," said Gamadge, laying down the *Quarterly* and finishing his cocktail.

"Well, he may have raided a country rectory or even a London terrace. Some degenerate descendant was hard up and couldn't resist the money. They need money over there."

"How about the well-known secret drawer in the old desk that couldn't be traced?"

"Oh, it wouldn't be fair to take that plot—that plot belongs exclusively to Henry James," said Coldfield. "What a problem for him, by the way. *H. James! Thou shouldst be living at this hour.*"

"But in no story of his would anybody have been allowed to sell letters."

"No, can't you see the terrific struggle of consciences? How glad I am that the Garthwain letters weren't sacrificed on the altar of common decency." Ames rose to fill Gamadge's glass.

Gamadge said: "The struggle would be understandable enough, if not the surrender."

"Well, not for me." Ames sat down again, his fresh cocktail in his hand.

"And you a man of letters."

"I know, I know."

"What possible harm?" insisted Gamadge, smiling.

"Mr. Gamadge, you shock me."

"The letters will certainly turn out to be interesting, to judge by the sample here; and all the Garthwains are dead, and the Garthwain connection wanted the money."

"You are simply taking the devil's side in order to start a controversy. Well, I'm good at these little controversies—I often take part in them in the literary reviews. But in this one I should sternly take my stand on the side of the angels. I feel very strongly in these matters, I admit it cheerfully. But nobody, you understand," said Ames archly, "is going to enjoy the Garthwain scandal more than I. I wish I knew how the sale was managed. My friend Salmon will be going over there this Summer, I should think he might find out something."

Gamadge had the sensation of being fed too much too fast, and he was choking on it. The *Quarterly* had been at his elbow, the landlady's daughter had been dangled in front of him like a stock figure of farce on wires, and now here was Salmon, his own suspect, being rammed down his throat. But after all: he himself had a copy of the *Quarterly*, and the landlady's daughter was a logical guess—Garthwain would never write any but literary letters to anybody—and Gamadge himself had introduced the subject of the discovery. As for Salmon, he came into the conversation honestly enough—he was suspect precisely because he was a bookish friend of the Coldfields'.

Ames Coldfield was in himself an enigma. From what Gamadge had heard of him and from what could be gathered about him on short acquaintance he seemed a thoroughly selfish and a far from benevolent man; and Gamadge thought he would probably be able to get a lot of fun out of an extra ten thousand dollars. And there must be a kind of hypocrisy about him too, a false kindness, or Sylvia Coldfield would never have confided in him. But Susan had said that with him it was "family, all family," and perhaps family was the passion of his life.

But if he had betrayed it—what kind of fix would Ames Coldfield have been in, if he had been found out as the trafficker in the letters to Serene?

He was chattering on: "Dear old Salmon, such a delightful fellow—he often picks up a bargain in books for me over there. Knows all the fellows in the trade, and half the collectors. I think he knows Locker. Did you know the letters were sold to Locker? Oh, yes indeed. Fellow I know on the staff of *Futurity* told me. Saw him when I was last in town. I seldom get to town these days, hate the crowds, hate the trains, and haven't my own car." He smiled at Gamadge, the cocktails were working in him. "As titular head of the family—only titular, the real head is the man that pays the bills, and Ira does that—I have as you see my own room; a room of my own." He laughed. "But not my own car. Well, I did get to town, and this fellow told me."

"Stupid of me not to take more interest," said Gamadge. "I ought to have dug that up myself."

"Yes, you really ought—it's in a way your business, isn't it—this kind of letter thing."

"Except that the Garthwain letters are authentic," said Gamadge.

"Poor Glendon," said Ames, putting his head back against the cushion of his chair and shutting his eyes. "I wish he'd lived to enjoy all this. How he would have enjoyed it. He must just have missed it, or he'd have mentioned it to me—the article, you know. Just missed it. I don't think the current issue of the *Quarterly* had been in the house long before he died. Wasted on Wall Street, Mr. Gamadge; a most intelligent man."

Gamadge mumbled something.

"Which brings us back to the problem of my sister-in-law." Ames suddenly opened his eyes and fastened them on Gamadge. "You mustn't be too hard on me, Mr. Gamadge. You really mustn't. You don't know how knocked over I was when she came in here and sprung that theory of hers on me. Really I was frightened."

"It was frightening."

"I mean I was frightened by her. I went into the kitchen hall to telephone to Smyth, and I confess that I hooked the baize door. I thought she had gone entirely off her head. Smyth was as shocked as I was; he's an old family friend, known us all our lives. Knew there was no record of any mental abnormality in the family, or in Georgette's—as far back as the records go, and they go pretty far. When he suggested a nurse for the present, I actually felt that it would be the kindest course to follow."

Gamadge said: "I still think your course was clear. The telephone call should have been to her psychiatrist, Dalgren."

"But we thought Dalgren had failed; how could we have confidence in Dalgren? And I really wish," said Ames pettishly, "that my sister-in-law had come to her senses at once, and that the whole thing had not ended on that note of rescue and escape. It makes us out—well, I'm glad you are having an opportunity to see us as we are."

"You must remember," said Gamadge, "that your sister-in-law's suggestion was offered to you in a spirit of kindness."

"Nor must you forget that if she had been herself the suggestion would never have been made."

Gamadge lighted a cigarette without replying; he was aware that Ames Coldfield's eyes were upon him, and raised his own, to meet a blank, fixed look; it was so consciously empty of all comprehension as to resemble the stare of idiocy. After a moment the pale eyes were turned away.

He knows, or he guesses, thought Gamadge, and said: "I confess my mind is irrevocably fixed on Mrs. Glendon Coldfield's desperate plight, and her lonely struggle to communicate."

"And how," asked Ames with sudden brightness, "did she ever do it? Those proxies? Did Miss Beal *not* look into them carefully before they were mailed? Well, it was kind of you to rescue her. And I hope Cook won't get a look at you through the slide at dinner—the gravy might get into the mayonnaise."

CHAPTER TEN

Serene

MR. AND MRS. IRA COLDFIELD came in from the library; Ira had put on a lounge coat, and Georgette was in dark-red and black silk, with a high neck and long sleeves. They made a handsome, prosperous-looking couple, without a care in the world.

"Got something left for us there, Ames?" asked Ira. He smiled at Gamadge. "Don't know where he gets his stuff, it's better than mine."

Ames was busy pouring from the big glass shaker. "And when I mix," he said, "I always expect company. Here you are, Georgy. Here you both are."

Georgette put a cigarette into her long ivory holder and Gamadge lighted it. She said to nobody in particular: "I see Jimmie dragged little Smyth in with him. Why in the world?"

"Well, after all, Georgy," murmured Ames, "it used to be a regular thing."

"It's the old man ought to be here," said Ira crossly. "We could do without the children."

"Doctor Smyth's grandchildren," Ames explained to Gamadge. "They always had the run of the house," he added. "Why not now? Because you're cross at Grandpapa? That's not at all fair."

"It's not at all true, either," said Georgette. "As you know."

"The boy didn't come," said Ira, who was getting through his cocktail in gulps. He held out his glass. "Thanks, old man."

"I never did care for the Smyth boy," said Georgette. "So rough."

"We can't have everything," laughed Ames. "He has the brains of the family. He'd better not go in for private practice—his bedside manner wouldn't soothe the patients, I'm sure."

"What's that old proverb or whatever it is," asked Ira, "about medical students and doctors? I myself always enjoyed talking to that boy."

"Well, we can't have all the neighbors underfoot now," said Georgette. "We have other things to do."

Gamadge said: "I think I've met a friend of yours, Mrs. Coldfield; of you all. Met him at a couple of auctions, but no more than a word or so. He mightn't remember me—he was busy."

"Who's that?" asked Georgette carelessly.

"William Venner, the Purchaser."

Ira said: "He isn't going to purchase anything here, and so I told him."

"No indeed," said Georgette, with a glance at Gamadge. "Not even that malachite table with brass legs in the drawing-room. I hope you saw that period piece, Mr. Gamadge? And the art nouveau floor-lamp with the Tiffany glass shade?"

"I was too busy admiring the gilt and glass tie-backs," said Gamadge.

"Oh, they're all right—they go back to Grandmother Coldfield," said Georgette. "But Bill Venner could have them if he wanted them, and all the rest of her stuff in the attic, to the last moth-eaten Paisley shawl."

"Moth-eaten?" Ira looked startled.

"Keep calm, dearest," said Georgette. "I'm speaking metaphorically. And I'm afraid Bill Venner wouldn't have the later bric-à-brac as a gift."

"Nobody's going to give him a thing," said Ira. "I won't have the carpets pulled out from under my feet."

"These Coldfields, Mr. Gamadge," said Georgette. "When they can't stand the sight of a thing any longer, do you know what they do with it? They put it away."

"People sometimes regret throwing things away," said Ames.

"Time enough to get rid of stuff when Susie's married," said Ira. "She ought to have her pick first."

"She'll pick enough to put in one suitcase," said Georgette, "the smallest suitcase in her set. And whatever she does take will come out of the attic." She held out her glass to Ames to be refilled. "I must say, though, the old dresses up there are rather fun. You get your hoarding instincts from her, Ira, of course. Grandmother Coldfield," she turned to Gamadge, "was so much in love with herself that she even got to worshipping her own possessions. She never threw clothes away. Trunks of them."

"Well, Georgy," said Ames, handing back the full glass to her, "as you said yourself, the things are amusing. I must say I get considerable pleasure out of all that bunched satin and velvet, and the thousand frills."

"I'm an antiquarian myself," said Gamadge, resigned to his new spate of free information. "If you'll show me the relics, I promise I won't try to buy any of them."

"Oh, there's nothing; they'd bore you," said Georgette. She finished her drink and walked off into the library. They followed her, Ira dodging ahead to push back the doors to the drawing-room.

Three young people were standing around the malachite table, on which was a tray containing a shaker and glasses.

Susan had changed to a pink ankle-length woolen dress; she turned: "Mr. Gamadge, this is Zelma Smyth—and Jimmie Waterton."

The slim girl who had worn the aquascutum with the hood was dressed in a yellow sweater and a yellowish tweed skirt. She was pale, with short dark hair, and she had a look of not much caring what impression she made. Her eyes were extraordinary—the blackest Gamadge had ever seen, and diamond-bright. She nodded shortly to Gamadge without speaking. Young Waterton was a fine-looking boy; big and blond, physically as hard as nails, and very friendly. He was wearing country clothes. He shook hands with Gamadge and smiled broadly at him.

"Susie says you're the tops, sir. Write, do you?"

"Er. You seem pretty well on the top of the world yourself, Mr. Waterton. Let me congratulate you."

"I guess you can." His hand went out to Susan's shoulder, but Mrs. Coldfield smilingly took his arm:

"Now let's just postpone it and come to dinner. We're all late."

They crossed the hall to the long dining-room, which had retained its pale old oak panelling and its faded, stamped-velvet wallpaper. There were portraits at each end of the room and between the windows; the one behind Georgette was a half-length of a stolid-looking man with flowing whiskers, the one behind Ira a three-quarter length of a woman.

Gamadge, sitting at his hostess's left, asked: "May I inquire who that lady was?"

Ames laughed. "He's fallen for her. That, Mr. Gamadge, is our legend—Serene. Mrs. Deane Coldfield. In fact my grandmother."

"Who was the artist?"

"Faulkner of London; not a particularly well-known man now, but Grandfather picked a winner, didn't he? I suppose somebody who knew told him to get that man and nobody else for Grandmother."

Gamadge let his mind wander into realms of fancy as he looked at the portrait. Had it been Garthwain who chose that artist? If so he knew what he was doing when he chose him. Grandmother Coldfield—but no grandmother in those days— had a rather long, delicately pointed face, questioning blue eyes, the smile of a wicked child. She was posed with her head tilted down a little and sideways, and the eyes were looking up aslant; she wore a little flowered bonnet on her curling hair, and the bonnet was set well back to show her deep curled fringe—it curled almost to her eyebrows. Her dress was a white veiling of some kind, with a square cut-out neck filled in with ruching. She had seed-pearl earrings and broad bracelets, and one hand rested on the crook of a lace parasol.

"Well!" said Gamadge, turning away as his soup was put before him. "She ought to have made that painter's fortune."

"I'm going to have those seed pearls," said Susan.

"And you can see the very parasol, if you like," said Ames, "in the attic."

"I shall insist."

Ames sat next to Miss Smyth on Gamadge's side of the table, at his brother's right. He said: "The trouble is, she lived too long."

"You know," grumbled Ira, "that kind of talk always goes against me. What can they do? Are we to take them out and shoot them?"

"But Ira," objected the titular head of the family, smiling, "think what a comfort it will be, when we know people are saying it about us, to remember how often we said it about people ourselves."

Waterton, opposite Gamadge on Mrs. Coldfield's right, said with a deferential look at Ames, "I don't know; I'm rather fond of Granny."

"Your granny, my dear boy," said Mrs. Coldfield, "is a perfectly charming old lady with lots of interests. My husband's granny was a horrid ex-beauty who had no interests except Patience—oh, those awful dog-eared cards!—and had to be carted to Greenbriar White Sulphur every Summer, and never opened her mouth unless she had a complaint to make or remembered some tiresome old scandal."

Ames was laughing. "She kept some myths alive. Poor dear, I always enjoyed her conversation. She was more amusing than Grandfather would have been at her age. And if any of us Coldfields have amusing qualities, James"—he addressed young Waterton benignly—"we get them from her, not from him. We needed her in our family."

The soup course was over, and Mrs. Coldfield turned to her future son-in-law. She and Susan and young Waterton were immediately in deep discussion—Summer plans, wedding plans, plans about a house that Waterton senior was going to build for the young couple on the estate, about a division of the camp in the Adirondacks. Ira and his brother seemed to have a subject of their own, the upkeep and final disposal of The Maples. Gamadge and his partner were left to entertain each other, and nobody paid the slightest attention to them.

She had been quiet and detached all along, saying nothing and not raising her brilliant eyes. Gamadge said: "Bad night to come out to dinner in."

"Yes, isn't it?" She raised the eyes to his. "The party was to have been at our place, you know. At Grandfather's."

"I didn't know."

"Just supper—just the four of us. Grandfather's away. When the plan was changed my brother wouldn't come, so I just...came...alone." Her voice dragged and ceased. If she had thought explanation necessary, she began to regret the impulse.

Gamadge said: "Some reason for the shift, I suppose; cook have a seizure? Refrigerator collapse? Bath water come through the ceiling? I'm remembering past calamities in my own house."

She gave him a bright unamused smile. "Oh no, but Susie didn't want to come out in the rain, and she hasn't been able to have anybody while her aunt was here sick, and they have a game room downstairs."

"But what happened to the chicken salad and stuff at your house?" asked Gamadge, reacting no doubt as she had hoped. She had spoken out of the bitterness of a burdened heart, and she had to go on:

"Lobster. It was just a buffet supper, and we were getting it ourselves—my brother and I were. The woman that works for us is out—it's her night off."

"Lobster for four and trimmings? That can mean a lot of fixing," said Gamadge, shocked.

"Oh well, Sam can eat a good deal of it."

"Hanged if I blame him for staying home for it. Of all the nerve," said Gamadge, his eyes on the couple opposite.

"Oh well, it doesn't matter."

"In my day it would have been called damn bad manners."

"Oh, it just happened; Jim wouldn't think—it wouldn't make any difference at the Waterton house."

"Susie Coldfield ought to know better."

"She wouldn't think either; it wouldn't be much fun down at our house, just playing cards, the four of us. They have darts in the game room. Susie likes to jump around on the spur of the moment, you know, not keep tied down to anything."

"That's a silly pose, old stuff."

"They have a little roulette wheel downstairs."

"I gather," said Gamadge, after they had done some eating in silence, "that the four of you are on pretty easy terms—old friends and neighbors?"

"Yes, we always knew the Watertons and the Coldfields. Our house is right in Cliffside village."

"Must be very pleasant up here in Summer—tennis, golf, everything."

"Sam and I haven't so much time any more. Sam's in medical school at Columbia, and Grandpa got me a job as receptionist in a doctor's office—three doctors, in fact."

"Shouldn't think you'd have time to eat, if you do all the appointments and everything."

"I keep the books, too; I had a course."

Another silence, which Gamadge broke: "Your brother was absolutely right; I don't know why *you* bothered to come."

"I had to; everybody knows Sam and what he's like, but if I'd refused—I think it would have hurt their feelings."

Their eyes met again, hers black and bold.

"People get absorbed," he said, "at certain times in their lives."

"Yes, but I wish I'd had time to dress."

"You were cracking those lobsters. Nobody really dressed, on account of me. I hadn't meant to stay for dinner."

"Oh, is that why Susie didn't dress?" She gave him the bright smile. "I rather wondered."

"Wonder not, nor admire not. Take things as they come, and if possible shoot them back."

"You're very nice, aren't you?" Miss Smyth sat back as Agnes removed her plate.

"Me? No. Not particularly."

"I don't see why Susie never mentioned you before."

"She never heard of me before. I'm a friend of Mrs. Glendon Coldfield's. I just came up to get some luggage for her."

She looked greatly surprised. "Oh—are you?" And as her dessert was put down, she asked, her eyes lowered: "Where is she?"

"Mrs. Glendon Coldfield? You a friend of hers?"

"I liked her very much; but of course she hardly knew me. I was sorry she had to go to the sanatorium."

"Your grandfather tell you about it?"

"Oh no, Susie did. He never talks about his cases. I just wondered where she's staying."

"Hotel."

Georgette Coldfield now turned to Gamadge again, but Miss Smyth was not taken into the conversation anywhere else. She sat quietly eating her frozen custard and fruit, quite ignored. She simply hadn't been able to stay at home among the ruins of her party. Waterton, the great oaf, thought Gamadge, was perfectly capable of thinking she would have a fine time up here; Susan had thoughts only for him. But the elders were not doing anything for the little Smyth girl.

Don't worry, thought Gamadge, she isn't going to get him back again.

But what a beating for her to take, just to be able to look at him now and then—without raising her head, an upward glance that he wouldn't notice or have to respond to. And she wasn't by any means the clinging vine type, either—perhaps he was her only weakness. She had a firm mouth—a little thin—and a good shape of head, and plenty of width of skull. Not a fool by any means.

Mrs. Coldfield was speaking to Agnes: "We'll have coffee here, Agnes, we'll be going straight down to the game room."

Gamadge said: "I mustn't get into a game, I have to dash for home no matter what the weather's like."

"The rain stopped, sir," said Agnes confidentially.

"Oh, has it? That's good. But Mrs. Coldfield, I was to have a look first at the relics, you know; up attic."

Ames asked, highly amused, "You really meant it? I'll take you myself."

"We'll all go up," declared Susan.

Zelma Smyth murmured: "Susie and I used to dress up in the clothes until they had to lock the trunks. I wore that dress lots of times." The motion of her head indicated Serene's portrait. "I couldn't get into it now; tiny little waist, and those slippers—there's nothing to them. I don't know how they stayed on."

"Perfect ladies didn't walk around in them," said Ames. "How glad I am, Mr. Gamadge, that you will only know her as she is there. She ended quite mummified, you know, and not quite a human piece of desiccation either: more like the remains of a bird of prey. Now Ira, don't frown, you know all about it."

Mrs. Coldfield rose, everybody rose. They went out into the hall and climbed the wide staircase—two flights and then they were in the upper hall. There was the third floor back, its door open, and another open door next to it; the Glendon Coldfield suite, empty as a tomb. No more Glendon Coldfields. What was the matter with all these people? They never even glanced that way, and only one of them was a murderer.

A big attic extended across the front of the house, with windows overlooking the drive. It looked tight and dry, and it was crowded with trunks, furniture and pictures: huge Saratoga trunks, little hoop-lidded trunks, heavy walnut dressers and chests of drawers, a towering headboard and footboard that had once been assembled into a double bed, pale-blue satin chairs and ottomans, engravings in pale-blue velvet frames. One dresser reached the low ceiling, with a full-length mirror between little marble-topped sets of drawers. There was a set of ornate steel fire irons and a painted fire-screen.

Ames stood in the middle of the place with extended arms. "Serene as she lived. Note the quart-sized perfume bottles, and the glove-box like an infant's coffin—to hold those long, long gloves unwrinkled."

Zelma Smyth had gone over to the row of trunks, and was trying the lid of one: "It's still locked."

"No, no," said Mrs. Coldfield impatiently, "that's full of junk of ours now."

Zelma opened another trunk and was pulling out lace and silk. Gamadge wandered along the walls, fingering loose objects. He came to a little rosewood writing box.

"This is nice," he said. "Better not let Mr. Venner get his hands on it."

Ames joined him. "What? Oh, the desk. Ira, here's the desk with Grandfather's letters in it."

Susan had been rooting in a drawer. "Here are the fans," she said. "Now they really are something, Mr. Gamadge. But what on earth is this?"

She was holding a cardboard box without a cover, and peering into it. Waterton came to look over her shoulder.

"Well, what do you know?"

"What is it, Jimmie, anyway?"

"Be a detective in ten easy lessons. It's a fingerprint outfit."

Everybody crowded to look. There was a little roller, a glass plate, a bottle of printer's ink and a bottle of grey powder; all neatly fitted in, and very clean.

Ames burst out laughing. "You remember, Ira, when Glen sent for it? All the rage, twenty-five years ago. He took all our prints, and the cook's and his own. Nobody came into the house but he got prints off them. Imagine his keeping it!"

"But why here?" asked Ira.

"Oh, things get poked away."

Gamadge was looking at the outfit in a kind of dream. Yes, Glendon Coldfield had got his evidence, all right; and then his wife and Gamadge and the cat Junior had gummed it up for him.

CHAPTER ELEVEN

Wrong Side of the Tracks

SUSAN PUT THE OUTFIT BACK into the drawer, and Gamadge helped her to close it. He was looking at the spangled, feathered, painted fans, when he heard his name. Turning, he saw Zelma Smyth peering at him over a crumpled, yellowing mass of furbelows. She was smiling like a conspirator.

"My dear child," said Ames, coming up behind him, "I beg of you! You look like Miss Havisham."

"They didn't get repacked properly."

"You try to do it," said Georgette.

Ira was laughing. "I think they must have been dressed up in once or twice too often," he said. "Perhaps we'd better get rid of the clothes, anyhow, Georgy."

"You think anybody'd want the musty things? I'll have Lefferts burn them."

Ames had opened the rosewood desk; it was packed with big, square, shiny white envelopes, tied up with pink tape in packets.

"Now here, Mr. Gamadge," he said, looking roguish, "I have a real treat for you. Grandfather Coldfield's letters to his wife, which—being intensely conventional—she preserved as you see. Glendon and I did have a go at them after she died, but we didn't get far. However, you as an antiquarian… You observe that there is no deception, I pick one out at random. I have entire confidence in Grandfather, and I am sure you will get the fine full flavor of him in any letter he ever penned."

Ames removed the closely written sheets of paper from the envelope, squinted at them and sighed.

"Old-fashioned man," he said. "Those silly long esses, and that deceptive flow that looks easy to read and isn't. Here we are."

He read in a mincing voice:

Paris, June fifth, 1880

My dear Wife:

I hope you are well and having pleasant weather at home. I had my usual attack of Cramps yesterday, after eating shellfish the night before; I had to dine with those men from the Bourse. But the Cholera mixture in the medicine case put me right.

I suppose you had better let Jenks mend the kitchen roof, but do not sign anything *until we see what happens after the Autumn rains. The estimate may not prove so reasonable after all.*

I executed your commission the other day, or did so as well as I could in the circumstances. You wanted twelve pairs of thirty-button white gloves and twelve pairs of openwork black silk stockings, but prices have gone up, and I am afraid that your dress allowance would not stand the strain. You must have calculated on the old basis. So I am bringing you six pairs of each…

Shrieks and howls of laughter drowned his voice. He looked up with an expression of hurt surprise, folded the letter, restored it to its envelope, and put it back among the others.

When he could be heard, he remarked smugly: "Grandfather in a nutshell."

"Oh, *poor* Great-grandmother," moaned Susan. "I hope she got even with him somehow."

"The type has its virtues," said Ira, still laughing. "He sounds to me like a very sensible man. An allowance is an allowance, after all, isn't it?"

"You listen to this, Susie," said Waterton, his hand in her arm. "Just what you need, perhaps."

"You ought to hear the struggles over *my* allowance!"

"Well, it was a good roof," said Ames. "It's still there."

"And now," said Gamadge, "after a very gratifying experience all round, I must really go."

Susan and Waterton shook hands, said it had been nice meeting him, and then rushed out into the hall and could be heard leaping down the stairs. The others followed, and were met by Agnes in the front hall.

"Mrs. Glendon's bags are in your car, sir."

"Oh, thanks, that's fine."

More handshaking, and then the three Coldfields went back down the hall while Agnes held open the door. Zelma Smyth had picked up her raincoat from a bench, and was behind Gamadge when he reached the car. He turned in surprise.

"You going already?"

"I ought to. My brother's alone there, and he has to work. I ought to tidy up for him."

"Let me run you down."

"Oh no, I can easily walk it. It isn't far."

"All the more reason for taking the lift."

"But it's out of your way."

"I'm in no such hurry as all that; I just didn't want to get involved in some game."

"Well, it's awfully nice of you."

He went around and opened the car door for her, and she settled herself. He came back, got under the wheel, and started off up the drive. The black route glistened wetly, there was a chill in the air.

After a silence, she said: "I hope it didn't look as though I was showing pique. That's so childish."

Gamadge kept his eyes on the road. "Pique? Why?"

"Because they didn't wait for me, things like that."

"Perhaps they're used to your independent ways."

She glanced at him quickly and looked away again. After another silence, she said: "I shouldn't have come. But Jim wouldn't understand it if I refused to go places with him and Susie; we've gone around together all our lives. But I don't think I will any more."

"That's right," said Gamadge. "You're not a parcel. He can't take you out with him and then forget about you." He added: "Funny thing about men, they can't see why they shouldn't keep old friends on very nearly the old terms—after they're committed elsewhere, you know."

"Women do," said Zelma dryly.

"Ah, but they know what they're doing, don't they? Well, everything fades at last."

Silence; her face was turned away. Presently she said: "We turn down here, Mr. Gamadge; it's terribly steep."

"I'll be careful."

As he made the turn, she said: "They're furious at Grandpa. Why did he run out on them like that? He wasn't meaning to go off for the week end. He took the car."

"I suppose a doctor—"

"This was just a visit."

They were descending a hill. She said after a minute: "Left here, please," and they entered a wide, dark street.

"Third house on the left. Don't bother to drive in, Mr. Gamadge, I—"

"Never dump a passenger." Gamadge drove between wooden gateposts, and stopped in front of an old frame house with a dim light showing through the fanlight above the grey door.

They got out. Zelma looked up at him to ask: "I suppose you wouldn't care to come in and meet Sam?"

"I'd like to."

She smiled. "You'd had enough of the party up there, too!"

"Enjoyed every minute of it."

Zelma rang an old bell with an iron knob. She said: "Perhaps it was silly of Sam and me to have a party, anyway. But Grandpa almost never goes away, and Sam and I wanted to do *something*."

"If we can't return hospitality, our position in the social scheme is precarious indeed."

"Ours is anyway," she said, laughing.

The door was opened by a thickset young man in slacks and a somewhat ragged cardigan. He was dark like his sister, wore spectacles, and carried a heavy book under his arm. He had some of his sister's good looks, but his reddish-brown eyes were without any particular lustre.

He said: "Throw you out, did they?", saw Gamadge, and stopped.

"Never mind Mr. Gamadge," said Zelma, "he saw them do it. He was very nice and brought me home; he's on his way to New York."

"Did you tell him he was headed for Albany? Of course there's the Bear Mountain Bridge, if he wants the ride."

"Don't be silly, Sam, he might like a glass of beer."

"I was going to knock off and have one myself," said young Smyth, looking at Gamadge. "Thanks for giving the kid a lift."

They entered a dim hallway; Gamadge and Zelma hung their raincoats on a hatrack, and followed Smyth along between sad-colored walls to an open doorway. Zelma led the way into a small study or library; a lamp with a green shade cast a circle of light on papers, notebooks, and a rounded object that looked like a grey old stone.

Zelma said: "Not that brain again. Take it right away."

Sam wrapped it tenderly in a cloth. "Such a good one," he protested, "I think it must have been donated by the owner."

"Dissection?" asked Gamadge with polite interest.

"Oh no, I'm not as backward as all that," said Sam. "I'm a third-year guy. Pathology." He walked to the door, his bundle carefully balanced on one arm. "Be right back with the beer."

Zelma asked: "Did you wash up?"

Sam turned. "Scraped and stacked till tomorrow."

"That *will* make us popular with Goldie!"

"Forget it."

Gamadge said: "I know how your sister feels. Let's all—"

"I wouldn't let you; but it would only take me a few minutes," said Zelma, looking apologetic. "If you really don't mind?"

"You know we figured it out that I'm not in a hurry."

Zelma laughed and went out with her brother. He came back carrying two open cans of beer and glasses. He poured, handed a glass to Gamadge, and said: "Why not sit down to it."

"Why not? Thanks."

Smyth lowered himself into a chair behind the table; Gamadge sat across from him, lighted a cigarette, and looked around him: old chocolate-colored walls, a Franklin stove in the old fireplace, a hole in the brown rug.

Smyth was watching him and smiling. "How do you like it across the railroad tracks?" he asked.

Gamadge raised his eyebrows. "Comfortable all-year-round old house," he said. "What's the matter with it?"

"You'd soon find out. Personally I like it fine, only I have to do a good many repairs in my spare time—whenever that is. Too bad the kid's upset; she used to be a nice girl till they ruined her disposition for her. Did they treat her very rough up there?"

"I thought the older people were rather rude; the others were oblivious."

"Zelma can't learn."

"I think she did tonight."

"I ought to have gone, I know it; somebody to pair off with down in the laundry."

"Where?"

"They call it the game room now; took out the stationary tubs and the gas stove and painted it blue, pink and green. Venner put in a good week end at it." Something amused him, but he repressed it. He said: "Trouble is, Zel and I ought to dress up more; then we'd look more like hangers-on and less like rugged individualists."

"Your sister complained that she hadn't time tonight."

"No, they came and swept her away. I dug my heels in—enough is enough. That foursome broke up for good." He looked up at Gamadge: "I seem to be talking somewhat frankly to a friend of the family, but from what Zelma said I got a kind of idea you were an onlooker."

"I am. I only came up to get Mrs. Glendon Coldfield's things."

Smyth now raised *his* eyebrows. "The mental case?"

"Sylvia Coldfield isn't a mental case," said Gamadge, looking surprised. "Far from it."

"That so?"

"I drove her down to New York last night. She's been with my wife and me—she's moving to a hotel. Charming person," said Gamadge.

"Yes." Smyth was regarding him steadily and with interest. "Grandpa slipped up on the diagnosis, did he? And is that why he took the car and beat it up-river as if the devil was after him? Well, he's a good family practitioner, but he knows even less about psychiatry than I do, and that's mighty little."

Gamadge said nothing.

Smyth, frowning a little now, went on: "Of course she was at the Dalgren place, but that needn't mean anything; it's used as a rich rest cure by people that can afford it—all the time. They go up when they're tired, or want a change from their families."

"So I understand."

"I always liked Mrs. Glendon, mighty nice woman. I'd have said she was a well-balanced personality, too." Smyth went on looking at Gamadge, his brows drawn together. "I didn't get the idea that there was any question of an accident with those capsules. Great Scott, don't tell me you think there was a mix-up in the prescription? There never was a word of anything like that." He added: "And Grandpa didn't have anything to do with that, anyhow." He went on slowly: "Zelma was there that evening—they were all having a quiet game of something in the laundry, they'd just had the bereavement, you know; you can't play anything really rough after there's been a bereavement."

Gamadge returned his smile. "No."

"The maid started yelling and screaming, and Zelma called the house here, and I got the message to Gramp. He was up there in a few minutes—in fact I drove him. I didn't go in."

Gamadge nodded.

"So of course the only place for her was Dalgren's."

"Yes. She got a clean bill of health there." Gamadge dropped his ash into a tray, and sat looking down at the end of his cigarette. "You might know more about this kind of thing than I do, Mr. Smyth. A stay in another kind of institution— mental institution, let's even call it by an old-fashioned name: insane asylum…"

Young Smyth was sitting quietly, his cigarette burning unheeded between strong brown fingers, his red-brown eyes on Gamadge's face.

"A stay in such a place," continued Gamadge, "following on the stay at Dalgren's; that would run up the record for anybody, wouldn't it? Even if the term of residence was temporary, the minimum thirty days? After that, the patient would have to be pretty discreet in word and deed, wouldn't you think so? Any other course of conduct wouldn't be taken seriously."

Smyth's cigarette moved a little between his fingers.

"I can't for the life of me see any sense in that thirty day arrangement," continued Gamadge thoughtfully, "except what I've said. And of course Sylvia Coldfield is no blood relation to the Coldfields, so why should the Watertons care about it? Nothing in the commitment to worry them."

Smyth ground out the end of his cigarette and sat up. "Listen," he said, "take my word for it: the old boy—Gramp—would only go along according to his lights. Perfect good faith. If he made a mistake, that's because these Coldfields have him hypnotized. He'd believe anything they said, he thinks they're holy writ. He and Old Man Coldfield—these people's father—were absolutely buddies—chips off the same block, too. If he ran out, well—he's old. He'd be embarrassed. I don't know what happened."

"Whatever happened, it's all over now," said Gamadge. "I mean Mrs. Coldfield's sanity is conceded once and for all."

"No trouble about it?"

"None whatever. Least said soonest mended."

Young Smyth sat back in his chair. He said after a minute: "That family's been the ruin of us."

"I wouldn't say so."

"That's because you don't know. Gramp made us keep in touch, when it was past a joke. It's done a few things to Zelma, let me tell you, and I'm not denying that it did a few things to me. But I'm older, I have interests. Don't get me wrong, Susie's all right; that mother of hers never let her have a chance to make anything of herself," he ended sombrely.

"She's very much in love."

"Yes, and Jim Waterton's a nice boy. He's stupid about human relationships, that's all."

The doorbell rang. They heard Zelma going along the hall to answer it, and then a chorus of voices.

"Don't tell me!" Young Smyth looked at Gamadge, grinning. "We have a couple of cases of conscience on our hands now."

Zelma, Susan Coldfield and Jim Waterton burst into the room. They were all talking.

"But I don't know what got into you, Zel. We waited and waited down there—"

"We thought you must be up with the family."

"And then they came down and we finished the game of ping-pong and Jimmie said—"

"And Mrs. Coldfield said you'd gone home."

"Did we do anything?"

Waterton had Zelma's arm in his grip; he was shaking it a little. Susan, in a loose topcoat, her hair blown by the wind, appealed to Sam: "She wasn't mad, Sam? Was she?"

"Mad, no. Just came home to wash the dishes," said Sam. "Are you two crazy?"

Zelma got herself free. "I just took advantage of Mr. Gamadge's invitation; he offered me a lift."

"Suffering cats," said Waterton, "I was bringing you home myself."

Sam looked as though he was enjoying himself. He was standing against the wall, hands in his pockets, smiling broadly. He said: "Us Smyths can't stay up all night, you know."

"But tomorrow's Saturday."

"Saturday means nothing to us Smyths. Don't you know yet what it means to be in training for the medical profession? Zelma has three doctors to look out for, and I have a dozen."

Susan clasped Zelma about the neck. "Come upstairs, I want to talk to you."

"Forget it, Susie."

"No, but I want to *talk*."

They looked at each other a moment, and then they went out and up the stairs.

"Sit down, guy," said Sam to Waterton. "I'll get you a beer."

"I'll get it myself."

"Go ahead, you know where it is."

"I ought to."

The big young man lumbered out. Sam and Gamadge exchanged a smiling look.

"And that's the way of it," said Sam.

"I'll just be going—they'll never know the difference."

"Don't blame you for lamming out of this."

His host walked with Gamadge to the car, and watched him as he drove away.

CHAPTER TWELVE

Report

CLARA AND MRS. COLDFIELD were playing rummy. When Gamadge appeared in the library doorway chairs went over backwards and a good many cards fell to the floor. Gamadge spoke over his wife's head in mild surprise:

"I know I'm late, but it was the only chance I had to look these people over. What's the excitement?"

"We were worried," said Mrs. Coldfield briefly.

"Your telephone call was so non-committal," said Clara, shaking him.

"It couldn't sound reassuring, with a member of the family at my elbow. I wasn't supposed to think they were a lot of gangsters," protested Gamadge.

Clara stood away from him. "Are you hungry?"

"Not even thirsty—yet. They gave me a very nice dinner. I left your bags in the car, Mrs. Coldfield, in case you really were determined to check out of here tonight."

"I can't make her stay," said Clara.

"Is it Mullins?" asked Gamadge, frowning. "Mullins the martyr? Pay no attention—"

"She's been very sweet," said Mrs. Coldfield.

"Henry doesn't like her," explained Clara, "because she said it wasn't sanitary to have cats around children."

"I'm only afraid it isn't sanitary for the cats," said Gamadge. "I'm perfectly sure Martin caught that child's flu once. Let's sit down—I have my report to submit to you."

They settled opposite him on the chesterfield, and he lighted a cigarette and looked at the ceiling.

"First of all," he began, "your lawyer Bob Macloud will meet the Coldfield lawyer whenever you say, and tomorrow morning I'll ring up and make an appointment with Bob for you. It's your husband's will—mere formality. You get it all, as you said. Nothing could be simpler or more sweet."

"I told you."

"Yes, money is no object."

"We couldn't believe it when you said you'd been asked to dinner."

"They made friends as soon as I told them you withdrew the suggestion about homicidal mania."

"Oh—of course." She was watching him anxiously.

"And I said there'd be no trouble about all that. Oh—the doctor wasn't there—had an engagement. His granddaughter was, though—later on—and she told me it wasn't a sick call, he'd gone off unexpectedly on a week-end visit."

"We might have known."

"Well, I didn't know him; but I can see it clearly enough now. He acted in good faith, trying to do what was best for the Coldfields, but he knew he was acting injudiciously, and he didn't suppose he'd ever have to defend his position. When he found that he *was* going to have to defend it, and to a layman with unspecified powers and perhaps a violent character, he simply couldn't face it. The Coldfields had got him into something, and they'd have to get him out of it as best they could. We can forget Doctor Smyth, I imagine."

"It's all pretty much as I thought," said Mrs. Coldfield.

"As for what they were planning in your interests," said Gamadge, "it seemed at first to present a problem: but I think I've solved it. You were going to be committed non-judicially to a private asylum, for the legal term of thirty days. After that your case would have to be reviewed by some kind of board, and they weren't having any of that. You'd have been turned loose, none the worse for it—I don't believe old Smyth would send you to any place of doubtful reputation."

"None the worse for it!" exclaimed Clara.

"So they would choose to believe. Thirty days of rest, quiet, mild therapy, 'observation.' Now I don't mean that all of them deliberately planned this to discredit you as a sane witness or balanced character for the rest of your life, I can't sort out the degrees of responsibility yet; but I think one or more of them did."

Clara said: "It's *worse* than murder."

"It's a kind of murder, yes, and we mustn't forget that one of them knew from the beginning that you had *nothing* against you—not even attempted suicide, which was the basis for the whole case. The murderer knew it. And let me assure you," said Gamadge, "that the murderer is as happy as a king. Or a queen, if queens are supposed to be happy too. Not a tremor, not a twitch of the nerves; that character feels as safe as a slug in a cocoon."

"If I used any such metaphor," said Clara, "you'd—"

"Never mind metaphors, or natural history either. Do I convey the fact to you?"

Mrs. Coldfield nodded.

"Now for what I did gather, which isn't much. Ames Coldfield knows as well as we do what our theory is; that you and your husband were given those capsules, with intent to kill. He's a clever man, as you said; a very clever man. He couldn't miss that alternative. Whether any of the others have missed it, I don't know. And I'm almost sure he knew those Garthwain letters were there in that little rosewood desk. Whether he simply found them, and left them, or whether he's the one who sold them, I don't as yet know. I'll know better tomorrow morning."

"Left them?" asked Clara.

"If he's the ancestor-worshipper he pretends to be (and may well be, in spite of his opinion of specific ancestors), what exactly could he do? Destroy them? That would be against all his instincts. Tell about them? I doubt it. If there had been a Garthwain affair there might have been others, and how would the Watertons, to say nothing of the family itself, feel about a suggestion of bâton sinister in the Coldfield arms? I think he'd leave them for the next generation to deal with, and meanwhile he'd savor the secret and get a lot of private fun out of it. I'm only guessing."

"And by the time Glen found out," said Mrs. Coldfield, "Ames had looked through the letters again; only one envelope was there. The Garthwain correspondence had been sold."

"Yes, he knows that too. So what does he do? Nothing. *He* had no evidence. But hasn't he wondered whether a criminal secret like that isn't connected with your husband's death?"

"He sounds very heartless and cruel," said Clara.

"In his way he is, I suppose. He gets a lot of fun out of it all—he got a lot of fun out of showing us the Deane Coldfield letters, and reading one of them to us."

"You actually got yourself up into that attic?"

"I did, but we won't go into it now—there isn't time. Now for your brother-in-law Ira Coldfield. He's an enigma, like all of his type; he's learned to control his feelings. He has outbursts at the right moments, but who's to say they're not calculated? There's nothing against his having seen the letters, and it's possible that he needed that money. The place seems to me to be a little understaffed, Mrs. Coldfield—or was, when you and your husband were part of the household."

"It was, of late years. Georgette seemed to find it hard to get servants up there."

"And that wedding is going to cost them plenty. On the face of it, he seems like the kind of man who'd take his brother's and his wife's advice about a case such as yours appeared to be; go along with them, perhaps reluctantly, entirely believing that you would be better off for a sojourn in a mental institution, unconsciously biassed by his own deeply felt wish to sweep you off the earth and out of the minds of men. I don't know.

"Mrs. Ira wouldn't be so likely to act without bias—would she?"

"No," said Mrs. Coldfield, smiling faintly.

"She'd certainly like to cut a dash in the eyes of the Watertons, and on her own account too. And there was a suggestion that she found her husband a little close with his money. Even Susan suggested it."

"He is, a little."

"He comes by it honestly," said Gamadge, laughing. "No question but that he's a Coldfield! As for Susan, she's very much attached to that eligible she's marrying. Nice enough fellow—I don't think myself that he'd bother his head about the shortcomings of Susan's ancestors. Did he have some kind of affair with the little Smyth girl before he took up with Susan Coldfield?"

Taken aback by the suddenness of the question, she looked at him, frowning. After a moment she said: "The four of them were always together; I suppose the Smyths more or less paired off with Susan and Jim. I never heard—"

"There's a family that needs money more than any Coldfield ever did. The boy is out—definitely out. He's on his own feet. This Zelma, though— She seems to have had the run of the house in the good old days before Susan's engagement, may keep to the old ways still. She knows that attic; and it wasn't she who found your husband's old fingerprinting outfit."

"There *was* one?"

"Certainly was, Susan dragged it out and didn't know what it was. Really didn't, I mean."

"He left it up there, after—"

"Apparently he did. Zelma Smyth was there the night you were poisoned, they were all playing games downstairs;

nobody'd be missed if they slipped away. How about the Sunday night—the night your husband was murdered?"

"But Mr. Gamadge—"

"Just tell me. Could she have been in the house that time?"

"Not that I know of. But—"

"The door that leads from the study, Ames's study, out into the garden. Is it kept locked?"

"No, not until everything's locked up at night. I simply can't—"

"She's lost Waterton to Susan Coldfield," said Gamadge. "She's not being treated at all nicely by the Coldfield people, they're afraid of her; and she isn't in a good state of mind about them. Susan and her James are not tactful. She may have lost him long before the engagement was announced, probably did; and if she found those letters, and knew what they meant in the way of money, it's just possible that she thought she'd be getting a bit of her own back without depriving anyone. And if your husband found her out, she'd be in a worse position than any Coldfield."

"That little thing! I don't believe it."

"But you didn't know her very well. There'd be books in Doctor Smyth's office that would tell her all about the amytal, wouldn't there? Perhaps there'd be amytal, too. We have to think of everything," Gamadge told her mildly. "And she was the only one of the lot that asked where you were."

"Zelma Smyth wanted to know where I'd gone?"

"Yes, but of course she says she likes you. We had a little of everything up there," said Gamadge reflectively, "including some uproarious farce, and a considerable amount of polite comedy, and a permeating sense of melodrama; but through it all, nobody asked me questions. Nobody but Susan."

"But Mr. Gamadge, what I don't understand is, who would act as Zelma Smyth's agent in England? Why do you even consider her, when you were so sure the agent thought it would be safe to sell the letters? You said a minute ago that she'd be in a very bad position if she were found out, the Coldfields wouldn't feel it necessary to protect *her*."

"That's a difficulty," admitted Gamadge, "and I'm pretty sure no agent of hers would find himself on your list. He'd have to be a big gambler—take a chance. But for reasons of my own I like her as a suspect—if I can be said to like anybody." He got up. "We'll know more about agents tomorrow. Now I'll just fix us up a nightcap, and then Clara and I will drive you over to the hotel."

"It's rather pleasant, by this time, to be sure that nobody knows where I am."

"You won't be lonely," said Clara. "I'll call up first thing in the morning, and we'll have lunch together."

Mrs. Coldfield sat back, looking up at them. She said: "I don't quote poetry, Glen broke me of it; and the only way I could possibly say what I feel about you two would be by quoting poetry."

"Don't have any illusions about us," begged Gamadge, laughing. "We do as we please."

"Even the animals get on together here."

Gamadge cast a dissatisfied look at the indistinguishable heap of tawny fur under the writing-table. He said: "Clara, won't you speak to your big dog again about licking my Junior? He'll have the fur off him."

CHAPTER THIRTEEN

Person to Person

NEXT MORNING Gamadge began the day by calling Macloud. When he got through to him he spoke in a sharp businesslike tone:

"Bob? Your client Mrs. Glendon Coldfield wants to have lunch with you at the Guildford if you can make it; one o'clock. She wants you to see her husband's executors—his brothers, the Coldfields—about his Will."

After a slight pause, Macloud asked: "You mean you got her out?"

"My dear good fellow, 'got her out'! What a ludicrous way of putting it. Would I ask a reputable lawyer to condone extra-legal proceedings of the kind you seem to imply? I went up there on Thursday evening, called for Mrs. Coldfield, and drove her to town. She spent the night with us, and last night she moved to the Guildford. Yesterday I went up there again—The Maples, Cliffside, you know, and had a talk with the family; you'd love them, just the kind of solid, respectable family you get on with.

I was sorry not to meet the family doctor, Smyth, you remember, but he didn't seem to care to meet me, for some reason, so we had to manage without him. You won't find anything but plain sailing about the Will; you're to meet the Coldfield lawyer if the executors decide that they'd be in the way. Rather retiring people, like all conservatives. Can you make it?"

Macloud said: "Don't be an ass. Wild horses wouldn't—"

"That's right. I won't give you the creeps over the telephone, Bob, Miss Murphy mightn't like it. But Mrs. Coldfield will. Do you mind if Clara's there?"

"Do I ever mind if Clara's there?"

"No. One o'clock, don't forget; and there'll be no trouble. Mind that."

"If you say so."

Gamadge rang off and called the office of *Futurity*. When the switchboard operator replied, he said briskly: "Hate to make a nuisance of myself, but could I ask a favor? This is Henry Gamadge speaking."

"Yes, Mr. Gamadge?" The young lady was distant and reserved with him.

"I wonder if you have a boy or perhaps a girl that you could send around to ask if anybody there knows a Mr. Ames Coldfield."

There was a silence; probably the young lady operator's mouth was open.

"And if anybody on the staff does know Mr. Ames Coldfield," Gamadge went on, "will you put him on the telephone?"

The young lady, after a pause, asked for Gamadge's name again and requested him to wait.

The wait wasn't long. A cheerful voice said: "Myers speaking. I've met Ames Coldfield—if that's what you wanted to know?"

"This is kind of you, Mr. Myers, and I'm ashamed to be such a bother and take your time. I only need a few seconds of it. I dined with the Coldfields last night, and Ames said you told him it was Locker that bought the Garthwain letters."

"Well, what do you know!" Mr. Myers was laughing. "It doesn't take long, does it? I saw the old boy at the Grolier Club doings, and I did mention Locker and the Garthwain letters, I remember it perfectly. I didn't realize at the time that it wasn't common knowledge yet over here—it was in England."

"You mean you told him recently?"

"No, last Fall—but before anything was printed here, you know."

"Locker wasn't mentioned in the *Quarterly* article."

"No, damn it, it seems to be a secret still, if you can call it a secret when everybody knows it."

"I didn't; I was greatly interested. Kind of an amateur book man myself. Did Ames tackle you about it? He would, if he thought you—"

"Yes, he certainly did; came up with his coffee-cup in his hand and button-holed me. Wanted to know all I knew about the sale—he'd heard rumors. I couldn't tell him anything but that—Locker bought the things. Fascinating, isn't it?"

"It is, Mr. Myers, and I'm much obliged to you for confirming it."

Gamadge, scowling, reached into his pocket, took out his notebook, and crossed Ames Coldfield off a list. Then he rang a downtown number, and was answered by a brisk and busy-sounding voice.

"It's Henry Gamadge, Mr. Geegan."

"Well, for Heaven's sakes, if it isn't! How's the boy?" inquired Mr. Geegan exuberantly. "Why don't I hear from you all these years? Don't you work any more except with police? How's Nordhall?"

"Fine, as far as I know, but we don't want any police in on this, Geegan."

"Getting out of line, are you?" Geegan laughed heartily.

"No, but it's confidential stuff—couldn't be more so. And I'm not even sure yet whether I'm going to need any of your people, or when, or exactly what for."

Geegan was delighted. "Sounds like you, all right."

"You're not as short of help as you were last time?"

"No, thank goodness, that was the war. I got a nice lot of young fellers now, veterans and everything."

"It's only a shadowing job, but the trouble is I may want the people right away."

"Full time?"

"Yes, and of course I'm engaging them as of now; two of them, if you can—"

"Wait a minute." Geegan was off the wire for several minutes. When he came back he said: "I can get you two, nice young fellows."

"Car?"

"Sure."

"Er—snappy dressers? They might have to go into restaurants and so on."

Geegan laughed again. "This isn't the war, let me remind you again. Bardo and Shaff, the names are; at least we call him Shaff because he's Polish, and his full name is something you wouldn't believe if you saw it written down."

"They're hired. Will you have them waiting around? I'll call up sometime before lunch. And Geegan—I don't know how long the job will last; will you get hold of a couple of night men for me too? I don't think I'll need them, but I'd better be prepared."

"No good taking chances."

"Just have Mr. Bardo and Mr. Shaff ready to go the minute I call, will you?"

"They'll be on one foot."

"Thanks, Geegan. You'll hear from me."

Clara came into the office, dressed to go out. "Any orders for the day?" she asked. "It's Saturday, you know; stores close early."

"I'm worrying about that a little. Clara"—Gamadge turned in his swivel chair to face her—"would you do a little job on the telephone for me?"

Clara said: "I'll be glad to. Those ghastly people."

"How did you know I wanted you to help out with the Coldfields?" Gamadge seldom asked her to involve herself directly in a case; he looked at her in some surprise.

"I knew by your expression," said Clara. "I feel very strongly about that whole family; you can say what you like, but even that girl—Susan—could have done something."

"No, she couldn't."

"She could. She was just too selfish to care. I wish," said Clara, coming over to the desk and laying her gloves and handbag down on it, "you wouldn't always make such an effort to be impartial, Henry. Sometimes there just aren't two sides to a question."

"Perhaps you're right." He got up. "I'd like you to call up the Cliffside place and find out somehow or other where the ladies are going to be today."

She stood looking at him. "You want them out of the house, do you?"

"I'd like to know their plans. As you said, it's Saturday."

"Then Ira Coldfield wouldn't be at work; and I suppose that creature Ames is always at home. Head of the family!"

"Ames didn't sell the letters, Clara."

"He didn't?"

"No. He wants to find out who sold them just as much as we do."

"How did you—"

"He's been asking around. He's not our man—forget him."

Clara sat down at the desk, looked at the number Gamadge put before her, and dialled.

After a pause she said: "I wonder if you could tell me whether Mrs. Coldfield and Susan are to be in town today?... Oh, they are? Thank you very much, I'll try to... No, that's all right, never mind, I won't bother to leave a message."

She put the receiver down. "It was the maid, Henry. They've started for New York, they'll be there all day. Agnes thinks it's lunch and a matinée."

"Thank you, it's just what I wanted."

"I'm disappointed, I rather hoped you were after Mrs. Ira. I feel very vindictive about her. But I suppose after all he's the likeliest. All that blustering yesterday!"

"We need some more of the whiskey," said Gamadge, "and some French vermouth."

It was a beautiful day. Gamadge, following Clara out of the house, stood with her for a minute on the steps as if he didn't like to part from her. "We ought to be doing something nice ourselves," he said. "I wouldn't even mind taking the boy, and some peanuts, and sitting in the park. Why don't we ever have a nice family party like that? And on Saturday we'd have lots of company."

"Are you crazy?"

"I just feel gregarious."

"It wouldn't be such a novelty for me, you know," said Clara grimly. "I've done plenty of that. I don't think you'd care for it. Let's leave it to Miss Mullins."

"It was only a dream."

She gave him a rather troubled glance, but he smiled; she walked away down the street towards Third Avenue and the markets, he turned in the opposite direction and hailed a cab at the corner.

The building was a big old business place on Madison Avenue, with retail shops for men's and women's wear on ground level, and a dozen office floors above. There was a double bank of elevators, with telephone booths beyond. Gamadge looked at the list of tenants, and spoke to an elevator man who was standing idle in front of his empty car:

"Mr. Venner in this morning, would you know?"

"Sure, he came in. Not much traffic Saturdays."

"No. Thanks. I'll go up. Eleven?"

"That's right."

"Wait a minute, I ought to telephone. I see some booths back there."

Gamadge went into a booth and telephoned Geegan.

"Shoot them right over, Geegan; it's not far." He gave the address. "His office is Eleven G. I'll be in there with him for a while, and I hope to get out before he does; if not I'll be with him, of course. The name's William Cole Venner, he's some kind of wholesale antique dealer, and I can't find his home address."

"They'll find it."

"I don't know whether the place has a back entrance."

"They'll find that out too."

"All I know is that he's about forty and supposed to be good-looking. If I don't have a chance to talk to your men, tell them to stick to him wherever he goes or whatever he does, even if he takes a train. They can report to me until after lunch, and then perhaps they'd better report to you and I'll call you."

"Fine. I get it."

"The whole thing may be a false alarm; if so, I'll try to let them know it. How on earth, Geegan, are they going to know me? I'm wearing a grey suit—"

"Don't worry," said Geegan, laughing, "they'll know you. I had some experience describing people."

"Shoot them over, then."

Gamadge went back to the elevators, stepped into another empty one, and was carried to the eleventh floor. He emerged into a cross-corridor, turned a corner, and walked between half-glass doors until he came to one marked G. A small gold inscription in the lower left-hand corner said: *William Cole Venner. Walk in.*

Gamadge walked in, directly into a room with big windows. There was thick carpet underfoot, heavy furniture—every piece declaring itself authentic to the most casual eye—and a row of big cabinets containing Sèvres and Saxe—more as decoration, probably, than advertisement of Mr. Venner's wares. A man sat at a desk under the nearest window—it was a handsome kneehole desk, big and solid like the other furniture. Mr. Venner dealt in no gimcracks.

The man looked up, rose, and came forward. He was as tall as Gamadge, a little heavier in build but not much; he wore dark London-made clothes and showed them off. He had light-brown hair, light-grey eyes, a long face with a squared chin, handsome features and a reddish, weathered skin. Deep lines ran from nose to mouth, aging him. He looked experienced, competent, tired, and rather dejected.

He asked: "What can I do for you?" in a pleasant but uninterested voice.

"I understand," said Gamadge, "that you buy things."

Venner looked a little surprised. "Well, yes, that's my trade," he said, politely taking Gamadge in. "I'm always interested in estates and libraries."

"You wouldn't be interested in mine, I'm afraid."

"If I come across something important I sometimes do a deal in the retail way," said Venner, "but very seldom now."

"As a matter of fact," said Gamadge, "what I had in mind was a swap."

Venner, more and more surprised, studied him. At last he said: "I never did go in much for that kind of thing."

"Too much haggling connected with it? There wouldn't be in this case. One price," said Gamadge.

They were facing each other, their eyes on a level. Venner had his hands in his pockets, and he was rocking gently back and forth on toes and heels. "What did you have in mind?" he asked, not without curiosity.

"I didn't bring the thing with me, of course," answered Gamadge, "but I can describe it in a way to satisfy you or anybody. It's a square envelope, bluish-white with just a hint of lilac. It has a red Victorian stamp on it, it's postmarked Shale, Somerset, 1875, and it's addressed to Mrs. Deane Coldfield, The Maples, Cliffside."

Venner had stopped rocking. Motionless, his lower lip caught under his teeth, he was looking at Gamadge without expression. An interval passed before he spoke:

"I wouldn't have believed it. I wouldn't, really."

"It must seem very strange," said Gamadge. "I ought to explain at once that there's no money involved in the deal."

"That makes me feel better, of course," said Venner, in the same flat voice. "What am I supposed to offer you in exchange for this object, then? I'm afraid I couldn't undertake—"

"I don't want you to sell any stolen goods for me," said Gamadge. "I only want the name of your principal."

CHAPTER FOURTEEN

No Deal

V ENNER DIDN'T MOVE or turn his eyes away; but after a short pause he suddenly took a hand out of a pocket; there was a cigarette case in his fingers. He opened it, took out a cigarette, felt in the pocket for a lighter, and bent his head to get a light. When the cigarette was going, he asked casually: "May I ask a question? It's legitimate when there's something of this kind offered for sale. Where did the envelope come from?"

"We know where it came from originally," said Gamadge. "From the rosewood box in the Coldfield attic. You'll be rather disgusted, I'm afraid—it seems to have been overlooked when the letters were taken."

Venner, his eyes on his cigarette and a faint smile deepening the creases beside his mouth, slowly and slightly moved his head from left to right.

"Where the other envelopes may be," continued Gamadge, "I don't know."

"I don't myself."

"So it's all I have to offer."

Venner put his head back to blow smoke. He said, his eyes on the cigarette once more, "Well, I'm afraid it's no deal."

"Don't be hasty. I should like to—"

"I'm not much interested. The fact of your coming here with this proposition means of course that you can't stir a step in any direction without my help. Well, that isn't at your disposal."

Gamadge said: "That's the proper first answer, of course. Let me try to make the bargain more acceptable to you. There is no threat implied."

"No? It isn't blackmail?" Venner smiled, more broadly.

"I shouldn't call it that. I know very well, Mr. Venner, that this wasn't a commonplace theft—that it was a family affair. I know it wouldn't be publicized, and that you're protected too. You must have felt very safe to take on such a thing. Perhaps you still are; I'm not trying to fix blame in the matter, it isn't directly important to me."

"No?"

"Not at all. I want the name of your principal for a different reason."

"What's that?"

"Are you sure you can't guess it?"

Venner looked him in the eye again. "Can't imagine."

"I'm inclined to believe that you never thought of it before; perhaps now you may. However, my position is this: the name of your principal will save me from the trouble of using that envelope to get the information elsewhere. I must get it, and if I have to use this evidence, of course I will. If I use it there will be an explosion, and you will probably be the first casualty."

"That's neat," said Venner admiringly.

"It's the situation. There's no trick about it—give me the name, and you get the envelope. It will be of no more use to me. I got it by accident, and I arrived at you as the agent by a clear process of reasoning."

Venner was rocking gently back and forth again, and he was still smiling. "You're not a blackmailer," he said, "but I'm still a fence—member of the criminal classes. We're notoriously suspicious. I get that envelope; what makes me think that you haven't photostatic copies of the incriminating object?"

"You don't seem logical, Mr. Venner. All I want is one piece of information, not more and more information. The envelope tells me nothing useful in itself."

"Sure enough." Venner turned on his heel, walked away to the farthest window, and stood there with his hand gripping the old faded brocade of the curtain: looking out at nothing. He swung round suddenly, and he gave an impression of a man elated. He came back to Gamadge, walking confidently, a brightness in his eyes. Gamadge watched him, frowning a little.

"I want twenty-four hours," said Venner.

"No. I must have the information by lunchtime today."

Venner looked at his watch. "That's putting the screws on. One o'clock? Less than three hours?" He turned his head away, seeming to calculate. "Can't be done under three hours, and that's final. And what do I do when I come to a decision? Leave a note for you in a hollow tree in the park?"

Gamadge took out his wallet and gave Venner a card: "No, you call me up."

Venner read the card, raised his eyebrows, and smiled. "I'm afraid I never heard of you. Is this supposed to convince me that I'll get the envelope in the mail?"

"Or you can call for it."

Venner burst out laughing. "I'll trust the mails."

Gamadge said abruptly: "Mr. Venner, may I advise you?"

"What else have you been doing?" The feverish gaiety was still in Venner's eyes.

"Don't consult your principal."

"What?" Venner stared. "You must be out of your mind to think I'd do such a thing. Isn't it the last thing I *would* do? I'm depending on you to cover up for me—isn't that the pact?"

"Then why the three hours?"

"Surely I ought to be allowed until half past one to wrestle with my conscience."

"Mr. Venner," said Gamadge, "let me earnestly beg you not to try a squeeze play."

"Squeeze play! I'm not a blackmailer either, you know," said Venner, laughing. "I stick to my own line of business."

"Your principal is tougher than you think; let me warn you."

"My principal and I will probably tell you to take your evidence and go to the devil with it." Venner was more and more amused. "You won't get far without us."

"Are you the only person who knows that name?"

Venner paused, looked at Gamadge with knitted brows, and then went off into shouts of laughter. Gamadge left him to it.

As he went out of the foyer through the revolving door, he was immediately aware of the good-looking, dark young man, well-dressed and slender, who stood just outside the entrance, smoking. The dark young man glanced at him, and then walked away from him into the next vestibule. Gamadge followed.

"Was it the party?"

"It was, Mr. Bardo—or is it Mr. Shaff?"

"Old Shaffsky's sitting in the car; got a place to park just around the corner, there isn't much parking just here of a Saturday. If the party comes out, duck into the store behind us and buy yourself a pair of socks."

"You can't miss him. He's about my height, medium coloring, out-door complexion, long squared-off face, lines from nose to chin. He's been around, and he's an educated man." Gamadge added: "Good clothes, so inconspicuous I hardly noticed them—a dark mixture, brown and something."

Bardo's glance at Gamadge was tolerant. He said: "I won't miss him."

"Have you plenty of money on you? I don't know whether I made Geegan understand—"

"Plenty. If he took a plane we'd have to wire ahead anyway."

"For God's sake don't lose him. I hired you to tail him, but now you're his bodyguard too."

"That so?" Bardo, watching the exit next door, received this news without visible surprise. "You don't want anything to happen to him?"

"I warned him myself, but he thinks he knows better."

Bardo glanced at him again. "You did?"

"Yes, but never mind that. Just hang on to him."

"Leave it to us. Anybody bothers him, Shaff and I we both carry our guns. Scares people," said Bardo.

Gamadge peered out into the street, emerged from his niche, and walked down to the corner. Rounding it, he saw a stocky light-haired young man at the wheel of a small blue car. Shaff gave him a brief smile, and raised one finger in salutation from the wheel.

Gamadge walked uptown to his garage, got his car out, and drove it home. He went through his office into the laboratory, hunted about there in files and cabinets until he found a leather case, sat down and opened it.

It was a legacy from Harold Bantz, when that all-around craftsman had retired into research chemistry and family life. Harold had demonstrated the use of the little implements within it, and Gamadge began to practise with them on the older type of lock in the laboratory and the office. He went upstairs and pursued his attempts there, ending with a successful attack on Miss Mullins's ancient steamer trunk. It bore some foreign labels, which Gamadge was sure she cleaned and varnished whenever they showed signs of wear.

He locked the trunk, looked around for other fields of conquest, passed over Miss Mullins's nice new suitcase, and went back downstairs.

Clara telephoned. Did Theodore understand that Gamadge was to have a nice lunch alone, since the latter wouldn't join the party at the Guildford?

Theodore did.

"Bob Macloud is here already, Henry, and they're having a wonderful time. I never in my life heard him laugh as much as he did when Sylvia told him about the rescue."

"He should have been with us."

"He takes it very seriously, Henry. He's dying to sue them for false arrest or something. Locking her up. We had to convince him that it was all over and done with; that part of it. Henry…"

"Yes."

"What are you doing?"

"At the moment?"

"No. About the rest of it."

"I don't quite know. I'm waiting for some information. I'm afraid I won't get it."

"Then what?"

"I'll take a little ride."

"Henry—"

"Forget it and have a good time."

"I'm terribly worried about your wanting to go and eat peanuts in the park."

"It only meant I didn't think I was going to enjoy my afternoon. Don't worry about me. Tell Mrs. Coldfield to remember what I said on Thursday night—about people tripping themselves up."

"I only hope they will."

"Signs point to it."

Gamadge had the nice lunch, and soon afterwards the telephone rang. He answered it in the library.

"You're punctual, Mr. Venner," said Gamadge.

"That's my reputation."

"And you sound happier than you ought to be."

"Quite happy. My answer is, publish and be damned. You know who said that?"

"The Duke of Wellington; to a blackmailer."

"I'm not surprised that you know; I've been looking you up. You're working for one of the others, aren't you?"

"Yes."

"I don't much think you'll explode any bombs, Mr. Gamadge. Too difficult in the circumstances to fix the blame.

I might be working for any of them, you know. Well, it was a good try."

"You've made it harder for me, of course. 'If I was to deny it, what would it avail me?' Who said that, Mr. Venner?"

"I don't know."

"Poker."

"Poker?"

"A young man of the name of Poker; a character who never got into the book that was never finished. A detective story."

"Well—what of it?"

"Dickens had to abandon him and try something else."

"Oh. Well, I'm afraid this mystery won't get finished either. I don't much care."

"Mr. Venner, let me warn you again. Don't let your principal take you for a ride, or make coffee for you in the solitude of the home, or push you out of a window. Beware of precipices, disguised blunt instruments and electrified bath water."

Venner laughed. "I'll be careful."

"Mr. Venner, I'm sorry to say it, you're a fool."

Gamadge had hardly replaced the receiver when the telephone rang again: "Mr. Gamadge? Bardo."

"Glad to hear from you."

"We didn't have any trouble with him at all. He came out and walked a couple of blocks over and got into his car—nice new one, Cadillac, all shiny."

"That could get away from you."

"If he was trying to get away. He won't see the necessity. He drove home—lives in the Francisco, nice old apartment hotel on Central Park West. He came out again a little before one—drove to Delorme's."

"He has good taste in restaurants."

"And money in his pockets. He waited in the lobby a few minutes, and along comes his date; good-looking dame, but middle-aged and filling out a little. Lots of make-up, touched-up hair, kind of a gold-brown. She has gland trouble—eyes beginning to bulge, throat thickening up. If I was her I'd watch it."

"You don't touch up your photographs, Bardo."

"Recognize her?"

"Yes," said Gamadge, "I'm afraid I do."

"She likes him, all right. She's a good dresser; fur jacket, little fancy hat that cost something, gold ball earrings. He had a table engaged. They sat right down to lunch, and in a few minutes he excused himself and went to a telephone booth outside the dining-room. I was in the next booth, still am. He was telephoning quite some time."

"Just finished calling me."

"That so! Well, he went back in the dining-room."

"Have your lunch there if you can get a table, Bardo."

"Shaff's trying for one. Anyway, we can see him from the line."

"Keep right at it."

"Want another report where you live?"

"No, I'll call Geegan. Make your next report to him."

Gamadge went downstairs, picked up his hat and topcoat from the chair in the front hall, and left the house. He got into his car and started for the third time on the trip north.

CHAPTER FIFTEEN

Ten Thousand

THERE WAS A PEARLY HAZE on the river this afternoon, and a rosy and amethyst light hung over the wooded banks towards Nyack like a premature sunset. The sky above the Coldfield house was filmed with cloud. A pleasant place to live, thought Gamadge as he turned into the driveway, but only if one was moderately happy.

Agnes greeted him at the door with a broad smile. "Mrs. Glendon's friend!"

"Yes, and I've come on another errand for her."

"Indeed we'll all be glad to do anything. There's not a soul at home, sir."

"Well, we don't need them. First of all," said Gamadge, taking a clean five-dollar bill out of his wallet, "Mrs. Coldfield wants you to have this for your trouble about her luggage."

"The nurse did most of it, sir. How is Mrs. Glendon, sir?"

"Perfectly well, she always was."

"There now."

"It was all a mistake."

Agnes received this familiar and all-sufficient formula with satisfaction. "We all knew it would come out like that."

"I'm back again because Mrs. Glendon thinks she left something she's going to need. A heavy coat."

Agnes looked doubtful. "There's her trunk, sir, we were going to send it on by express on Monday. But—"

"She says she thinks it's in a trunk in the attic. A big locked trunk; if you'd go up with me I could find it."

Agnes was astonished. "But that trunk has Mrs. Ira's old riding clothes and Mr. Ira's fishing boots and things in it."

"Mrs. Glendon is pretty sure her coat is there. Couldn't we just look?"

"Yes, sir, of course. But I haven't the key."

"She had one."

"She *did*, sir?"

"Yes, I can open the trunk. But first might I telephone?"

"Certainly, sir."

"And meanwhile you might just make sure that there's no heavy coat in Mrs. Coldfield's trunk, you know. I'll join you."

Agnes left him to go upstairs. Gamadge sat down at the telephone and dialled Geegan.

Geegan sounded amused. "Hello, where are you?"

"At Cliffside-on-Hudson. Here's the number." Gamadge supplied it. "You can get me here for the next hour, say. But I'll try to ring you before I leave."

"I might be ringing you myself, the subject is moving around."

"Is he?"

"They sat a long time over lunch, Bardo says; then he said a fond farewell to the lady, and got in his car and drove uptown— to Yorkville."

"Yorkville!"

"Yorkville, way over east; to a little beergarden, the Schönbrunn, between Second and Third. Sawdust on the floor, checked table-cloths, one waiter, and the garden is out back; has the fountain in it too, all correct—dwarf made of lead, pouring water out of a beer-keg; only the water isn't running today."

"Picturesque," said Gamadge.

"I guess that's the idea. The place is empty this time of day, Bardo says there's nobody in it but the subject and himself, with Shaff parked outside a little way down. The subject is parked at the table beside the one window, enjoying a beer. Bardo's trying to make his last—he's back at the bar, end of the room. But after a while he'll have to leave, sit in the car."

"Couldn't he go quietly to sleep in a booth?"

"He will, that's his idea, but he won't be able to stay forever. Well, looks as if we might have some more to report pretty soon, don't it? I'll say goodbye now."

Gamadge rang off, climbed the two flights of stairs to the top floor.

Agnes came into the hall to meet him. "It's not there, sir. I thought sure I put her tweed coat into her big case."

"This seems to be another one."

Agnes preceded him into the attic, and stood gazing blankly at the Saratoga trunk in the corner near the window. Gamadge said: "Just see if any of the others are locked, would you?" and walked up to the monster with its great hasps and its iron bands. He bent to the lock, and after a moment it snapped open with a click that brought Agnes to his side.

"That's the one, sir, sure enough."

"Seems to be." He raised the lid. Both of them stood gazing down at a carefully packed top tray.

Agnes said faintly: "Is them hers?"

"You don't recognize anything?"

"Never saw them in my life. That's mink, isn't it?"

"Here, let's get some of the stuff out."

"This trunk here is dusted," said Agnes, giving it an extra wipe with her apron. Gamadge piled garments one after the other into her waiting arms: a full-length mink coat, a short white-fur jacket, a set of silver fox, a pink costume trimmed with bands of beaver. He lifted the tray out, and delved further down.

"Shot-silk dress," he said. "Cocktail dress, would you say? Boy, look at the label. Here's an evening thing, gold and silver. Summer dresses. And underneath, sure enough, at the bottom, the riding clothes and boots, and Mr. Coldfield's waders."

"Can't you find Mrs. Glendon's coat, sir?"

"No. Here, let's get these things back again."

Agnes, panting, folded them. "But who do they belong to, sir? Mrs. Glendon never—"

"How much would they be worth, should you say, Agnes?"

"My God; I don't know."

"Just look at where they all came from; I've heard my wife say a thing or two. And those furs—and the coat. As near ten thousand dollars as makes no matter, minus perhaps a little something for expenses."

Agnes straightened to look at him, a thought striking her: "It wouldn't be Miss Susie's trousseau, sir?"

"Well, don't they seem to have been worn?"

Agnes nodded, and replaced the last of them in a daze. At last she said: "Lock it up good, sir, it's supposed to be safe against the moths when it's locked."

Gamadge pushed the hasp of the lock in, and snapped the side fastenings. He said: "Mrs. Glendon made a mistake. No mink in her philosophy."

Wheels sounded faintly on gravel. Agnes went to one of the low windows and looked out. "It's a cab—Mr. Ames has come home."

"Good. I'll go down with you and meet him at the door."

But Gamadge withdrew into the drawing-room while Agnes let Ames Coldfield into the house. He replaced his key in his pocket, spoke to Agnes, and then looked up and saw the visitor standing just beyond the doorway on the left.

His coat half-way off, Ames stared.

"Glad I waited, Mr. Coldfield," said Gamadge.

Ames, slowly removing the coat, spoke even more slowly: "Mr. Gamadge. Did we expect you?"

"No, I came up for a word with you."

Agnes looked puzzled, took the coat, and retired with it and Ames's hat to the back of the hall. Ames said: "Always glad to see you, of course," and led the way back through the drawing-room and the library to his den. There he turned. "Anything special that I can do for you?"

"Special, yes."

Ames walked over to the French window, and stood looking out. He said: "Curious and beautiful light effects at this time of the year; but I always think there's a desolateness about the early Spring; the chill in the air." He stepped back a little, and moved to the cupboard on his left without looking at Gamadge. "A little brandy?" he asked.

"Not for me. You might not care to offer it to me when we've had our talk."

Still with his back turned, Ames got out a decanter and a glass, filled the tiny bell, and drank the brandy off. Then at last he faced Gamadge, but kept his eyes averted as he came over to the hearth. He bent and touched a match to the fire.

"Might as well be comfortable," he said. "No need to sit freezing. Well, Mr. Gamadge." He straightened up, the cold blue eyes were on Gamadge's now. "More trouble about my sister-in-law?"

Gamadge met the stare with one as cold. "I bring it to you as head of the family. Poetic justice, Mr. Coldfield." He put his hand into the side pocket of his coat, and brought it out with a folded paper in it. "If you hadn't betrayed her when she came to you, if you'd accepted her word and allowed her to go, this"—he laid the blue envelope on the table between them—"would eventually have been lost or thrown away."

Ames leaned over to look at it. When he raised his head, his face was mottled, patched with red; the face of an old man. He said in a whisper: "If it's her revenge, it's an ugly one."

"You still underrate her," said Gamadge. "She'd never use it as you seem to think she would."

Ames pointed at it. "Where?" he asked, searching Gamadge's eyes.

"It was in her husband's crossword book."

There was a long silence. Then Ames said in a different voice: "I see."

"Where the others are, she doesn't know."

"We know where the letters are," said Ames dryly. "And it's due to my own cursed folly that they weren't destroyed." He had recovered himself a little. "I more or less gather that you exonerate me in the matter of the theft?" His smile was only a slight grimace, twisting up a corner of his lip.

"Yes. You seem to have wanted information about the sale yourself…"

Ames watched him, always with the smile.

"And I have other reasons for exonerating you."

"I am sure you have." Ames suddenly struck the table with the flat of his hand, turned away and sat down in his chair before the fire. He clenched the hand and spoke hurriedly, in a thin, angry voice: "God Almighty, the women the Coldfield men marry and cherish—the unspeakable women they bring into this house! You know Serene's quality now. My mother, poor lady, was colorless. But this—this—" he glanced at the envelope on the table and looked away—"this perhaps excuses me for wondering at the time whether Glendon's wife wasn't another of our strange women, bent on disgracing us. Can you—" he looked at Gamadge pleadingly—"can you understand why I wasn't quite fair to her when she came to me with that story? I'd seen those Garthwain letters, and then when I looked into the box after I read that *Quarterly* article, they were gone. I don't mean I thought *she'd* taken them. No indeed."

"I suppose you couldn't bring yourself to destroy them when you first found them?"

"Couldn't, simply couldn't; as a man of letters, you know," said Ames.

"It was a responsibility."

"Vandalism—I couldn't bring myself to it. What I feebly tried to persuade myself was that Susan would inherit them, and throw them out unread—unfound—as rubbish. At least the responsibility wouldn't be mine. I left it to destiny—but destiny never manages things as we foresee. Well, when next I looked for them they were gone, as I said; and having read the article, I knew where."

"And you couldn't guess at the agent?"

Ames struck the table again. "Who knows what friends a woman like that picks up, or where she finds them? She's always at my poor brother for money, you know; on whom does she spend it? I dare say she'd find good use for the proceeds of this sale. I don't know what Serene's honor brought in the market."

"Ten thousand."

Ames put his head back to stare. "Ten thousand! Well, that's high. I imagine that Garthwain wouldn't think so."

"It would have been more with the envelopes."

"That—" Ames pointed to the blue envelope again—"you mean it's at my disposal?"

"Unless you feel the need of it as evidence."

"But what kind of evidence do I need, more than I have?"

Gamadge sat down in the other chair. He asked: "Mr. Coldfield, do you really mean that you never realized until last night, while we were talking, the possible truth in Sylvia Coldfield's story?"

Ames didn't answer; his jaw sagged a little, his fingers played with the blue envelope, that idiotic stare had come back into his eyes.

"Your brother knew all about the Garthwain letters," said Gamadge. "He'd read them, he'd left them, he read the article in the *Quarterly* and went and looked for them again. They were gone, and he knew where too. But he had evidence against the thief, and later he had proof. Do you remember that fingerprinting outfit?"

Ames nodded vaguely.

"There are no prints on that now," said Gamadge, indicating the blue envelope. "It's had careless treatment. But he found them there the day he died. Sylvia Coldfield was right—but she was too merciful. There is no insanity in your family, Mr. Coldfield."

Ames stammered: "Last night I—but I cast it out of my mind. Fantastic."

"So your sister-in-law, Glendon's widow, thought. But when she thought so, she didn't know about the Garthwain letters."

Ames suddenly got to his feet. He said faintly: "I must have some brandy. I…" He went to the cupboard, and came back with the decanter and two of the little glasses. His hands were trembling. He filled the glasses, sat down and began to sip at his own drink. After a minute he cleared his throat, and said more loudly: "Motive, yes. No proof now."

"But evidence—lots of evidence. Don't you want to hear what it is?" Gamadge, his elbow on the table, was leaning towards him. "Your brother's widow won't use it; but don't you think the rest of you ought to know that there's a poisoner under your roof? Do you think that with such a murderer there may never be a next time? And the next time you might have police in the house—and they'd search more than the attics."

"Attics?"

"Mr. Coldfield, last night Zelma Smyth tried to open a trunk; your brother Ira's wife said it was full of old things, and that it was locked. This afternoon I unlocked it. It isn't full of old things—it's full of valuable furs and dresses, things that Agnes didn't recognize. They cost very nearly ten thousand dollars, or I'm much mistaken."

Ames said, his voice quivering: "She's mad for dress."

"But what opportunity would your brother's wife have for wearing those things?" Gamadge paused. "You're an intelligent man, Mr. Coldfield. Think! Don't blind yourself through prejudice. How could she do it without your brother's knowledge?" He sat back slowly. "It was the agent that interested me from the first, you know."

Ames nodded again, still vaguely.

"I didn't see any other approach," said Gamadge. "If I followed up your lead about Myers and the Locker information you wanted, it was purely from a sense of duty—Mr. Salmon didn't seem a likely prospect to me. The agent of course had to be a man of standing and reputation, apparently good for the ten thousand dollar guarantee, or those English people wouldn't have listened to him; but what man of standing and reputation would take such a risk? No matter how safe the agent felt, there is always a risk, and it was ruin for him if something went wrong. Did he need money? Nonsense; such a man wouldn't do a thing of that kind for the whole ten thousand, or half of it, or any commission you care to name. No, something else came into that deal. Why did his principal trust him so absolutely? Why did he violate all business and personal standards of honor? I thought he'd behaved like a man in love.

"But even a man in love wouldn't presumably act unless he felt safe, and he wouldn't have felt safe unless the Garthwain deal was protected by family sentiment. The principal in this affair would in case of trouble be protected by the Coldfields, and that probability cut out everybody but a member of the family, at least for me.

"The agent must be a man of business reputation then, but a man who couldn't afford to *give* his principal ten thousand dollars. He couldn't have afforded therefore to pay back the ten thousand himself; was he less prosperous than he seemed?

"Of all the family friends I had heard of, Venner seemed least unlikely to fill my requirements. He was comparatively young, therefore perhaps comparatively adventurous. His business is not so stabilizing as some others, he might still be riding on his father's reputation. He knew the Coldfields, what they're like and what they'd do in certain circumstances. He's unattached, has only himself to think of; he and his father before him must have had long-standing relations with English men of business, and they'd often need the services of a solicitor. He's extremely good-looking; a love affair wasn't by any means unthinkable. I've seen him, Mr. Coldfield—he's a man of experience and a very attractive one."

Ames mumbled something.

"He doesn't deny it," said Gamadge. "He's our man. Mr. Coldfield, you're a man of experience too. Would Venner be likely to underwrite a deal in stolen goods for love of a middle-aged married woman, who's losing her figure and her looks and has nothing to give him but herself? She hasn't much to give a man like that. She probably wouldn't be able to bring much alimony along with her if she left your brother, would she? Do you think she'd get anything? Mr. Coldfield—I'm trying to prepare you."

Ames moved his shoulders in a gesture of refusal.

"Let's imagine," said Gamadge, "that Venner swung the deal for a young girl who had fallen violently in love with a most eligible young man. The competition must have been gruelling—no doubt she was as far out of his financial class as Zelma Smyth was out of hers. She must go on visits, go to important parties, travel, keep herself in his eye. He was young, and she knew how likely his affections were to wander."

There was a shrinking motion of Ames's shoulders.

"Her father couldn't give her the really large sums she needed," continued Gamadge, "but she chanced upon a way to help herself—with the help of a friend. She bought what she wanted, and she rented a place in New York to keep the things in, to change in—perhaps to meet the friend in? But she soon threw him over, and what could he do about it without implicating himself?

"She got her man. She could manage now without the new clothes, and she would be glad to get rid of the expense of her room in New York. That trunk was never opened—she got the things up here and packed them away until she could smuggle them out somehow with her trousseau when she was married. After that, who would question her possession of them?"

Ames was shaking his head, more as if in despair than in negation. His hands gripped the arms of his chair, his eyes were fixed on the fire.

"This morning," said Gamadge, "for the first time, Venner saw a chance to get her back. I gave it to him. I described this envelope, and I offered it to him in exchange for his principal's name. I said that if he didn't give me the name I should have to use the envelope to get it. He thought I meant to use it in England, where he'd underwritten a deal in stolen goods to the tune of ten thousand dollars; but I wasn't going to use it in England. I was going to use it here, to get that locked trunk open if I had no chance at it myself. I thought by what your sister-in-law said about it last night that it would be a pretty safe hiding-place for the rest of the Garthwain envelopes. But after that discovery of the fingerprinting outfit in the attic I was afraid there'd be no prints on those envelopes now."

Ames lifted his head suddenly to look at Gamadge with a sort of pale hope in his eyes: "But my niece found that outfit, and she didn't know what it was. Had no idea at all."

"You noticed that? So did I, and I can't say it didn't influence me at the time. But later on I asked myself why she *should* know what it was. We have no idea of course what your brother Glendon told her about the proof he had against her, and she had no knowledge of his fingerprint set—it was brought into the house and played with and discarded before she was born. The box had no label on it, the outfit looks as much like some kind of utility desk equipment as anything else. There was ink, there was a little roller like those roller blotters you used to see, and inkpads are used for rubber stamps. If she didn't notice the bottle of powder—but what if she did? Do you suppose that Susan Coldfield reads the kind of literature that familiarizes people with fingerprinting?"

"No."

"At first glance she wouldn't know it; then she would wake, and remember, and understand. But your brother Glendon," said Gamadge, "wouldn't like me to quote poetry."

Ames didn't hear this. He said in bitter reminiscence: "I noticed, but I wasn't concentrating on Susan. I was watching them all. Why do you think I performed those antics, Mr. Gamadge? Took you up there at all?"

"I had some idea that you were under a compulsion to demonstrate your own innocence—not especially to me."

"I wanted to find out who the criminal was. I wanted to frighten and disturb the criminal. I wanted evidence to take to poor Ira. Now—now—" he stopped, drank brandy, wiped his lips. "Am I to tell him? This Venner: what—"

"He couldn't deny having been the agent in the sale of the letters," said Gamadge. "I took him by surprise at first, and then he had to know what I was after; he couldn't find out by showing me the door. But he knew that if I had the proof I wanted I shouldn't be there talking to him, and he asked for time. He wanted to consult his principal, and he did consult her. He had to find out where she was from her mother, with whom he was lunching in New York."

Ames glanced at him half furtively.

"He'd want to keep in touch with her family," said Gamadge, replying to the glance. "Why should your sister-in-law refuse a date with a personable man? But Venner was interested elsewhere. As soon as he found out where Susan was lunching, he called her and got her promise: to return to him in payment for his silence. They arranged to meet later in the afternoon.

"Did he know what he was asking? He realized that it would be a frightful wrench for her to give up Waterton and her marriage and all the money; he knew he wasn't offering her much in the way of a future. There might not be proof against either of them, but they were going to have a lot of trouble first and last, and if her family didn't stand by her she and Venner might be very hard up indeed. But he only wanted Susan Coldfield, and she had loved him once; perhaps she might love him again.

"But she's as much in love with Waterton now as Venner is with her, and she knows something that Venner doesn't; she knows she may be facing an inquiry much more serious than an investigation into the sale of the Garthwain letters. By this time she has no illusions about what's behind my investigation—and she can't tell Venner. She's in a trap."

Ames had his head buried in his hands; his voice came as if from a distance: "Hard as stone. All of us in the family knew it, but an outsider like Glendon's wife wouldn't. She could be very charming. It will be Ira's death."

The telephone rang, and Gamadge stood up. He said: "That might be for me. Shall I go?"

Ames made a slight, indeterminate gesture, and Gamadge went out into the hall.

The voice over the telephone was Bardo's, but Gamadge could barely recognize it; Bardo's aplomb was shattered, he was gasping:

"Mr. Gamadge—"

"Yes. What—"

"Geegan said I was to call you myself, explain we couldn't help it."

"Is it Venner? What happened to him?"

"My God, he's killed a woman."

CHAPTER SIXTEEN

Warning

BARDO GOT NO ANSWER. Recovering his breath, he spoke louder: "You hear me, Mr. Gamadge?"

"Yes, go ahead."

"Mr. Gamadge, I can't believe it yet. I'm here at Geegan's, he wanted me to call you right away; tell you myself. I've had the shock of my life, and Shaff has too, and we've seen some things. But this—well, here's the way it was.

"We were right there at that beer joint, me at the back in a booth, Shaff outside in the car, off to the left of the entrance, reading a paper. The subject is sitting at the table in the window, making his beer last and smoking.

"Pretty soon along comes a very swell-looking young dame, she's on foot. I'd say she dismissed her cab at the corner. She's in her middle twenties, streamlined, riding high, she's—"

"I know who it was, Bardo."

"It's a comfort to me you know anything about it. Well, the subject got up and went to the door to meet her, and Shaff will bear me out that there was great enthusiasm on both sides. They came in and sat down, he's facing my end of the room; and his face was all lit up. I was thinking you couldn't very well pick out a more private spot to meet anybody in than this little joint in Yorkville.

"A waiter got their order—*the* waiter, I should say—two beers. Good bitter stuff they serve there, I was enjoying mine. I was acting half asleep, hat pulled down and all like that, you know. I could see she wasn't settling herself there, she was in a hurry. He argued it, but no, she couldn't stay long at all. He had two beers, she'd only drink one. He hadn't more than started on his second when she called for the check, and she fairly made him gulp the second drink down. Then he paid, and they started to go, and she actually had him under the arm urging him out. Talking to beat the band. He laughed, but he seemed to see it her way, she was saying something about her train.

"They went across the sidewalk to his car, and she shook her head, no, she was getting a cab. I suppose she meant she couldn't be seen with him. Anyway, he opened the door and he got a foot inside. I was paying my check by this time, but I saw it all. He stopped, half in and half out, as if he'd suddenly thought of something; and she kind of gave him a little shove.

"He backed out and turned his head and looked at her, and he had a smile on his face as if something had put him wise. And then he had his two hands on her neck, and before we even knew what he was doing…it was Judo or something, unarmed combat, what they learned in the war; a little jerk and a twist, and her head snapped back and she was down on the sidewalk like a bag of sawdust."

Bardo sounded as if he wanted to cry: "Right on the street, and I thought they were such friends. I was running, the waiter was ahead of me, the bartender was coming around the counter. Shaff was half out of the car, but Venner was back behind his wheel, door slammed, driving away. Shaff took after him. I merely ran. People were yelling now, the Third Avenue light was against him, he'd never get far, and his bus was weaving as if he was drunk. I figured, let the cops do the shooting."

"Yes," said Gamadge.

"You said it was confidential, but of course we'd do what was necessary if we had to. We didn't have to, Mr. Gamadge. This Venner was out of his mind, all right—he tramped on the gas and straightened out, and shot his car right into the traffic on the avenue. You never saw such a…you'd have thought he was doped."

Gamadge said something.

"What?"

"Go on."

"I could hardly look," said Bardo. "You never saw such a smash in your life, he must be in pieces. That El pillar; a bus hit the tail of his car, a big truck rammed him amidships. His car turned over. He was—I faded into the crowd."

"Right."

"You think so?" asked Bardo anxiously. "Geegan—"

"Absolutely the right thing."

"I figured you might want it that way. Cops' whistles were blowing by that time, and I got in the car with Shaff and sat till we were moved along. By the time we travelled round the block and back through the street again, she'd been covered up with some newspapers and a bystander told us—there was a big crowd by then—that the wagon was coming. We didn't know whether you'd want more information about the two of them?"

"No, the assignment's over. Tell Geegan so, and you get your full time."

"Well, thanks, Mr. Gamadge. Thanks. Perhaps you can make head or tail of it."

"Perhaps. Goodbye," said Gamadge, "and thanks for calling."

He put the receiver down and walked slowly back into the study. Ames sat waiting for him, and greeted him with an inarticulate question and a frightened stare.

Gamadge came up to the table, picked up the little glass of brandy that had been ready for him so long, and drank half of it. He said: "It's all over, Mr. Coldfield. She's dead."

"Thank God."

"Venner killed her."

Ames seemed to collect his faculties. "Do you mean—will it all have to come out? Even now?"

"I'd better tell you what happened, then you can judge for yourself. I had two men watching him, as much to protect him as anything else; he met her in a little restaurant, and she seems to have saved out twenty grains of the amytal and somehow managed to get it into his drink. She thought he'd drive away in his car and die in it, or in a traffic accident. Nobody at the restaurant would ever connect such a death with him or with her. But she still didn't quite realize how fast that stuff works. You'd think, after Sylvia Coldfield's experience—"

Ames said with a touch of his old dryness: "They'd spare my niece some of the details."

"Anyhow, she thought she'd get him started off in his car. I think he might have made it—far enough to answer her purpose; but I'd warned him. He felt that something was wrong with him, he remembered what I'd said, and he thought he was a dead man. In that moment he may even have believed what he hadn't allowed himself to believe before, that she was a poisoner already.

"What poison? He didn't know. He was going out fast, but he had time to strangle her and drive away. He drove into the traffic on the Avenue—he was doped and dying, only knew enough to keep his foot down. Venner would never try any such ineffectual form of suicide as that."

"But was he—"

"If he wasn't killed, he must have been badly smashed; he'd die of the amytal before they ever thought of anything but shock and perhaps internal injuries. There'll be no autopsy, Mr. Coldfield, or if there is, they won't look for sleeping medicine. There'll be a terrific scandal, of course, and the case will be closed—a love affair, jealousy, an insane getaway. That's all," said Gamadge. "Her father and mother may never know that it might be worse."

Ames got himself to his feet. "You won't tell them?"

"There's no reason for me to tell them now. Your niece isn't a danger any more."

Ames looked down at the blue envelope: "You say you were looking for the others in that trunk?"

"Yes, and they may be there—safe enough. I don't believe she ever put them through the formalities of a safe-deposit box; a court order can get even a safe-deposit box opened. She may have destroyed them; last night I must have made her very nervous—anything out of the ordinary troubles a guilty conscience, and of course she was always nervous about Mrs. Glendon Coldfield. *She* would have let her go and been glad to see the last of her."

"Georgette has the key of that trunk. I—" he looked cloudily around him. "I shan't rest easy until they're found."

"Well," said Gamadge, "at least you can get rid of this one."

Ames stared at him, picked it up, and faltered: "Don't you—as a man of letters—hesitate...?"

"I don't feel that the shade of Mrs. Deane Coldfield needs any further appeasement."

Ames grimaced, tore the envelope into fragments, and cast them on the fire.

Gamadge left him gazing down at the charred paper in the grate, got himself out of the house and into his car, and drove away. What, he wondered, would the girl's wretched parents make of those clothes in the locked trunk? Years from now, perhaps, they would be found. Presents from Venner? And what would his client make of Susan Coldfield's end? But Gamadge knew that, of course. Tripped herself up, but who shoved her?

"They'll all wish they could give me a decoration," he told himself, "and nobody will ever dare to say so."

CHAPTER SEVENTEEN

Pathology

SOME MONTHS LATER Gamadge was waiting in a downtown bar for a would-be client to meet him and show him an autograph letter.

"I guess it's the real thing," the client had said on the telephone. "But it's only signed 'Garthwain.' It's just a few lines, thanking some old guy in our family for sending him his umbrella—he lost it on a London bus. It's been kicking around the house for years. We thought since this boom it might be worth more than it would have brought earlier."

"Double, I should say," Gamadge had told him, "and the poet often signed himself 'Garthwain.'"

"Well, if you could meet me on my way home from the office—have to take a train home, but I said I might be late."

So Gamadge waited, leaning up at the bar and absorbing an old-fashioned. He noticed four young people in a booth who were having a fine time; two men and two pretty girls. One of the men detached himself from his party and came up to the bar.

"Mr. Gamadge: you wouldn't remember me."

"Mr. Smyth. How are you?"

"I'm all right, thanks. Mind if I talk a minute?"

"I don't know how you can bear to leave your friends over there."

"Especially the redheaded one?"

"I've been admiring her."

"Mrs. Smyth, if I ever get my degree."

"Congratulations; that's good news."

"Zelma and I had a little windfall, aged aunt died."

"I don't think I ought to condole, in the circumstances. Tell me if I'm wrong, though," said Gamadge.

They were both heartless enough to laugh at this sally, and Gamadge ordered more drinks.

Sam pondered over his for a minute. Then he said: "Lots of changes since I saw you last."

"Yes."

"Coldfield house shut up. Gramp retired and lives in Florida. Zel and I have a little place in New York." He had turned grave. "Gramp was shaken up by what happened, you know. More than we were. Zel and I got a little away from all that, you know; but Gramp—what I wanted to say was, I think he finally caught on to the capsule mystery."

Gamadge looked inquiring.

"So did I," said Sam. "Not at the time—impossible for me to guess. You must have thought me pretty dumb that night you were at the house."

"Far from it."

"Of course I don't know any details," said Sam. "Only the ones everybody knows. But I suppose Glendon Coldfield and his wife somehow got on to that affair with Venner. Zelma knew about it when it was going on."

"Really?" Gamadge was interested.

"And she told me after it all came out." Sam looked down into his drink. "She's pretty good about keeping secrets— Zelma is, I mean. Susie told her all about Venner, she was crazy about the guy for years, but she wouldn't marry him because he didn't have money. His business had gone down after his father died. He was a man that had to live a certain way, and he spent too much. So Zelma understood."

"I had an idea that he was like that."

"Because Susie wouldn't marry him? Anyhow, she left his letters with Zel after she got engaged to Jim Waterton."

"She did? Why?"

"I don't know, she was like that," said Sam. "Pathological, in a way, like wanting Zelma around after she got Jim Waterton away from her. Wanted me around, too, but not feeling about Susie the way poor old Zel felt about Waterton, I wouldn't play."

"So I gathered," said Gamadge.

"It all made me very sore. What did you think about the two of them coming down that night to apologize?"

"I didn't understand it."

"First I thought it was some more pathology, but Zelma told me after the tragedy—Susie came down to get those Venner letters back."

Gamadge straightened, drank some of his old-fashioned, and lighted a cigarette. Then he asked: "That so?"

"Remember she made Zelma take her upstairs?"

"I remember, yes."

"The letters were in a little locked-up case Susie had, and it went into a pocket of her topcoat."

"Very interesting."

"She was going to have some kind of a showdown with him, I suppose, and it ended by his killing her. I felt very sorry for that unfortunate guy," said Sam.

"I feel sorry for Waterton, too."

"Oh, old Jim will recuperate. They're all abroad, you know, Coldfields and Watertons, all of them. What a bust-up, wasn't it? I'd come to realize that Susie was as cruel as the grave, but I—still, you only had to look at that portrait of her grandmother in the dining-room to realize that the subject was a psychopath."

"There was a cruelty there, yes. And you didn't think Susan's mother's influence was good, did you?"

"Well, no. But Susie was all right when we were children. At least I thought so; you never can tell what's going on in the human brain."

"I wish you'd give your sister a message from me, Mr. Smyth."

"Glad to, what is it?"

"Tell her I think she's admirable."

"Oh—you mean because she didn't give Susie away about Venner?"

"She had some provocation."

"Oh, Zel would never do that."

"I have the highest opinion of her."

"I'll tell her. You might like to know that she and the youngest doctor in her outfit are getting along quite well lately."

Gamadge was pleased. "I'm glad to hear it. I was rather afraid young Mr. Waterton would come around again."

"Afraid? That's good." Sam laughed aloud.

"I know he's very nice, but he's really too thick in the head."

"He did come around, and Zel was very sympathetic with him. But somehow that last night—well, I won't annoy you any more." Sam finished his drink and they shook hands. "Just quietly remember me to Mrs. Glendon Coldfield if you see her."

"She'll like to hear from you."

"That's the worst thing Susie ever did."

"Only there's no evidence."

"She could have read up on her subject in Gramp's office."

"Let it go."

"Anything you say."

Sam went back to his party. A small man came in with a commuter's rush; he was carrying a brief case, and as he stopped and glanced about him he took a square, bluish envelope out of an inside pocket and held it tight in predatory fingers. Gamadge couldn't bear to look at it.

Want more Henry Gamadge? Read the first two chapters of the next—and last—mystery in the series, *The Book of the Crime*

CHAPTER ONE

Dog Walkers

A GIRL AND A DOG came down the steep brownstone steps; the dog in short, frog-like leaps (he was a Boston terrier, large for his breed), the girl holding on to his leash with one hand, to her cap-like hat with the other. It was a dark, cold April day, six o'clock in the afternoon, and she pulled her fur coat around her when they reached the sidewalk.

She would have turned left to Madison, but the dog preferred the long stretch to Fifth—the Austen house was near the Madison Avenue corner. She followed, indifferent. Rena Austen did not care for the dog Aby, he was the only dog in her life that she had never liked: his brindled coat always felt hot and damp to the hand, his hindquarters hung loose on him and waggled disagreeably at a gesture or a word. He was a sycophant and a coward. But she realized that she ought to feel grateful to Aby, since he was her excuse for getting out of the house and away from human company at this depressing hour. By human company she meant that of the Austens; she seldom saw anybody else.

That narrow house! Squeezed between two others like it, with only a sliver of front showing, but so much of it extending back and back to the limits of the lot. Just a sliver of yard beside the kitchen, and Aby wasn't allowed *there*. The cook would soon have him out of it with a broom.

Dark narrow rooms, dark stairs, dark corners. A perfect trap to her eyes, but plenty of space for a family of four, and too much, she would have thought, for the old gentleman who had lived there and had willed it to Gray Austen, her husband. But the old gentleman had had a family once, she supposed. Now she and Gray had the second-floor back suite; Gray's brother and sister, Jerome and Hildreth, had the third floor; the servants were above. Just right for comfort.

What was wrong with them?

Aby, as usual, kept her waiting on the Fifth Avenue corner in the chill wind, while she looked at the letter box and thought that she had nobody to write to. The only friend she had had in New York, the only one to whom she could possibly write an intimate letter, was married and abroad. And even if there was anybody to write to, what could she say? It would sound well, the kind of thing she had in mind! It would be a nice thing to tell anyone. "My husband was an airman, he will always be lame from a war wound, he walks with a brace. I met him on a bench in Central Park, while I still had that good job you got me; I fell in love with him, and we were married in a month. That was about a year ago. He had plenty of money, because his uncle left him an income for life, and an old house here; he and his brother and sister came on from Oregon to live here, after the war. I have everything, and I had nothing and nobody. I wasn't a child, I was nineteen years old—it was a love match.

"And in three weeks—three weeks!—I decided that we had both made a fearful mistake."

Aby consented to be dragged away from the lamppost, and trotted ahead of her along the avenue, snuffling.

Seven weeks, thought Rena. People didn't behave like that—fall in and out of love in seven weeks. Gray said they didn't, and denied it so far as he was concerned—absolutely denied it. He wouldn't let her even mention it. But he had made the mistake too, whatever he said; she must have been as deceptive unconsciously as he had been—that melancholy, beautiful young man with his braced leg; his dark eyes had looked so kind. But he was far from kind, and his moods were so black that sometimes she felt afraid of him.

It was vulgar to tire of a marriage in a year. What could anybody think, but that she had married for what she could get out of it, the alimony? And a lame man, a war hero too. It was out of the question.

The registrar had been so nice; it had really been very solemn. Rena had meant never to leave Gray Austen, and perhaps "for better, for worse" meant that people must get over their whims and stand by their bargain, and not try to get out of it on the excuse that they hadn't understood what they were letting themselves in for. Rena's whim had lasted a year. "Oh, if it were not for Aby," she thought, as they turned east at the corner, "I needn't go back into that house again. But I could shove him inside when Norah opened the door, and just turn around and go."

Go where? Live on what, until she got another job—if she ever did? "I know Gray would never let me have a divorce, and what respectable person would help me to get one?"

Was it their idleness that made the Austen family so tiresome? None of them did anything. Jerome and Hildreth lived on Gray, Gray lived on his income. There was an excuse for him, and he'd gone into the war so young that he'd never had any other kind of work at all. But Jerome had been an accountant in Portland, Hildreth had had a position outside Portland as a librarian. Hildreth, the eldest of them, wasn't more than forty; but not one of them seemed to have the slightest intention of doing anything again for the rest of their lives. Hildreth pretended to run the house, but they had inherited all of old Mr. Austen's servants, and *they* ran the house—Hildreth didn't spend an hour a day on it. Jerome lolled about, ate and drank, amused himself.

The others of course could fill up their time as Gray couldn't—they got around, picked up friends, went to plays and concerts and exhibitions, travelled; flitted back and forth between New York and Portland to settle the family affairs. They'd just come home from that last trip. But Gray—wouldn't any other normal human being find himself something to do? He didn't suffer at all, he was an intelligent, well-read man. Well, that brought it all back to the original trouble and question—Gray's case. He was simply one of those cases, she supposed, and his problem wasn't that he couldn't dance or play golf or tennis, lead an active life; it came from the effects of the war itself on him, and his recovery would be difficult and slow. She was there presumably to help him; and all she could think of was getting away.

At first she had wondered whether his first wife's death had been what he couldn't recover from; but after he told her about it, before they were married and indeed almost as soon as they began to talk at all intimately, he had not referred to it again. Nobody talked about the first wife, and why should they, to her? A sad subject—Gray had married her here, very soon after he got his discharge and came to New York early in 1946. They were married two years, and then she had died of virulent pneumonia, there in the Austen house. Gray had stood his loneliness for a year, and then he had met Rena in the park.

Two years! The first Mrs. Gray Austen had lasted two years, and the second Mrs. Austen didn't look like lasting for more than one. Had the other girl been so worn down by boredom and hopelessness and strain that she couldn't put up any resistance to the disease? Such a nice little thing she had sounded like, a hostess in a restaurant: Gray couldn't exactly be accused of fortune-hunting! Pretty, with Rena's light colouring, and as isolated in the world as Rena was.

The wretched Aby tried to stop at the Madison Avenue corner, but Rena wouldn't let him; mean of her, she thought, but he was such a dawdler. A big dog on a short leash was coming along the street, paying no attention to them, but Aby got behind her. "He can't help it," she thought, feeling angry because the man with the other dog laughed at Aby and at her. The big dog ignored the whole thing. Traffic streamed or jolted past them, cabs and buses taking people home. Huge trucks ground by, horns blew. Not many pedestrians, though, at this hour with the stores closed. Just dog walkers, in hot weather or cold, rain or shine.

She had followed the old track again, the course of the sign that stood for infinity; around first one loop and then the other, back to where the lines crossed: the walk with Aby always just got her back to where the lines crossed. Here they were near the last corner, and then there would be the big apartment house to pass, and a house, and then the Austen house. Would they all be in the library waiting for cocktails as usual? Or would they be down in the front basement, knocking balls around on the old pool table—mixing the cocktails themselves at the bar? The liquor was all down there, and so Gray was down there often. Not that he exactly *drank*, Rena protested to herself; at least he carried it all right, but it seemed to make people short-tempered instead of gay. In the long run, of course.

She and Aby were passing the service alley of the apartment house now, and Aby was always interested in garbage cans. She let him stop a minute to fuss and sniff there in his unattractive fervent way, with her eye out for superintendents and porters; but they never seemed to be around at that hour. Suddenly he glanced over his shoulder, started violently, and disappeared behind one of the cans; Rena almost lost her grip on his leash. A voice said: "I just wanted to apologize."

She looked around and up; the big dog's owner was big too, big and tall, with a tweed overcoat hanging open and a soft hat in his hand. The wolfhound's leash was wrapped around the other hand, and his collar gripped firmly in gloved fingers.

"Gawain wouldn't hurt a fly," said the hound's owner.

"I notice you have him pretty tight," said Rena, responding to the man's smile with one of her own.

"Well, he might nose up a little. Leave your pup where he is a minute, if he likes it there; I wanted to explain—I didn't laugh to be rude or anything."

"I know Aby's funny, but he can't help it."

The big man was youngish, and his face had a skin-grafting job all the way down his left cheek. He had tawny hair; he looked at her from lively blue eyes, half-closed.

"That's his name, is it? I know him from before the war," said the big man. "What I wanted to explain. He's getting on, poor old guy. Many a time I used to meet old Mr. Austen walking him, when I was walking the pup we had then—police dog it was. Old Mr. Austen and I had many a good laugh over this Aby. So today I—didn't mean to be rude."

"Perfectly all right," said Rena. "I suppose I'm a little touchy about him."

"Don't blame you. The best dog we ever had—best pedigree, I mean—he wasn't quite right in the head. Bull terrier, and up in the country he used to come home otherwise all right, but with the tip of his tail pretty nearly bit off."

Rena hadn't heard herself laugh for so long that she startled herself now.

"My name's Ordway," said the young man. He jerked his head backwards: "We live across the street there. Always lived there, since this region was built up—I mean the family has. Austens too. I understand there are Austens there again."

"Yes, I'm Mrs. Austen."

"Oh. Yes." He glanced at her briefly. "He caught it worse than some of us. I've seen him out walking the pup. I suppose that's your husband."

"Yes, Gray."

"Well..." Conversation halted. Then the young man said politely: "Got to be getting on with this brute, he needs more of a stroll than yours does."

The wolfhound had stood all this time like a statue, his chin up and his eyes fixed on nothing. Rena said: "He's beautiful."

"Yes, nice feller."

Mr. Ordway smiled at her again, replaced his hat, and went off up the block. Rena unwound Aby from the garbage can, and followed at a distance.

As she and Aby climbed the front steps of the house, she hoped the Austens were down in the basement; if they were in the library Aby would rush in, and somebody—Jerome or Hildreth—would call to her. That was routine. They didn't like her, she was sure they thought Gray a fool to have married her, but they put up a show. Gray said it was her imagination. Even the servants ignored her as much as they could. And how they adored Gray, all of them! Rena had a good idea of the kind of thing they said in the kitchen: What a little nobody of a gold digger, to catch Mr. Gray, God love him.

The front door opened finally to her ring—Norah would have been in the basement getting the cocktail tray ready. The wrinkled Norah admitted her glumly; Aby dashed past for the library. Jerome's voice called to her in his patronizing way: "Hello there, Chick, come on back."

If she didn't, somebody would come upstairs after her. She left her coat and hat on the hall bench and went along the passage past the drawing-room on the right, past the basement stairs on the left, through the little dark square ante-room with its book-cases surmounted by busts of Roman worthies, into the big library.

It was always in a half-light, since one of its high windows was blocked by the house next door and one was inset with medallions of German stained glass. The open dining-room doors beyond sent in most of the light there was. Now in the dusk, with no lamps on and a low fire in the chimney-place, it was like a cave. She could hardly make out the three figures sitting around the hearth.

Hildreth's affected voice said: "Turn on a lamp, will you, pet? And join us. Almost time for cocktails."

CHAPTER TWO

Two Ways Out

NOBODY MOVED as Rena came and stood beside Gray's chair. He was lounging far back in it as usual, his braced leg out in front of him, cigarettes on the little table that would hold his cocktail and his canapé, a book in his hands. He looked very morose, and didn't lift his face to look up at her. His dark eyes were fixed on the fire.

Jerome sat in the middle chair, with Aby slavering at his feet: Aby knew that bits of toast and perhaps bacon would soon be coming his way. A hateful, conceited fellow Rena thought Jerome was; tall, dark, heavy and getting heavier, with thick jowls and a slightly overhanging upper lip. He had none of Gray's beauty or charm, but he had personality, no doubt of it. Hildreth was lighter than the others: rust-coloured hair and eyes, a sallow, freckled skin, shallow jaws, an ungainly figure; her feet were clumsy, yet she always crossed her knees and had one foot out as if to be admired.

Jerome and Hildreth were talking about their trip home to settle up a deceased aunt's estate. Rena, looking down at her husband, wondered how in spite of his sullen moods she had ever fallen out of love with him. His narrow, pale face was so appealing, clear and regularly featured as a statue's; his eyes so beautifully set, his mouth so firm, his hair so smooth and fine. What was he reading? *Her* book—one of the few she owned. She kept it up in their sitting-room, and she didn't remember that he had ever noticed it.

She remembered very well how she had come to buy it. She thought of the day in the publisher's office where she worked, the day she had been sent into the editor-in-chief's room with a manuscript. The author was there, and several other people, and as she came towards the door she heard them all laughing. When she went in she saw that they were laughing at something the author had been saying; he was leaning up against the window ledge with his hands in his pockets, a colourless-looking man except for greenish eyes. If she could have expressed the impression he made on her, she would have said that he was entirely without self-consciousness or arrogance, but quite sure of himself; and that he was kind, but got a lot of amusement out of his fellow-creatures.

His manuscript was entitled: *Murderers Speak*.

"Thank you, Miss Seton," said the editor from behind his desk.

The author had thought it was "Seaton." He said: "My God, Miss Seaton, I hope you have no aunt?"

Somebody asked: "Now what? Why shouldn't she?" But she had answered him seriously: "It isn't spelt that way."

Then they had both begun to laugh, and he had said: "Miss Seton, I am your friend for life. Shall we send these people to night school?"

"I just happened—"

"I happen to read Walter de la Mare too. You tell me if an aunt or anybody else bothers you."

She had hurried out, smiling; and of course she had asked about him in the office, and they had told her a good deal. She had bought his book when it came out, and had enjoyed it very much. Gray never read such things, though; he never read all the interesting crime books up in their sitting-room. The bookshelves were crammed with them, trials and novels, old and new.

Hildreth was saying: "...and really, Gray, there's something to be said for a stiff knee. If it doesn't hurt, I mean."

"Think so?" Gray's eyes turned towards her, the whites showing.

"Alibis you out of anything."

"That's so," agreed Jerome. "*You* don't have to travel across a continent to collect seven hundred and fifty dollars and crate up a houseful of stuff that nobody wants. But you'll be paying part of the storage on it, my boy."

"Seven hundred and fifty all she had?" asked Gray without interest.

"I told you; she lived on the interest out of a trust fund, and the principal now goes to village improvements. I don't know how she ever saved the seven fifty, hanged if I do."

Hildreth remarked: "I can send for the stuff, Gray, if you ever get sick of me and want me to set up in a place of my own."

Gray said with a dryness unusual to him where his brother and sister were concerned: "I don't think Uncle's bequest would run to two establishments."

"Darling Gray, you know I was joking. And as a matter of fact some of that furniture isn't bad."

"Wouldn't fit in here," said Jerome, looking around him and smiling.

Gray said: "Throw it out as far as I'm concerned. This may be as bad as you and Hil say, but it suits me.

"Bad but fascinating," said Hildreth, "and very comfortable. Oh, the wonderful beds."

"Thank God Uncle liked you, old boy," said Jerome.

Nobody was paying any attention to Rena—did anybody ever? She went quietly out of the library, along the passage, and up the stairs.

It was a steep flight, and at the head of it, just before the turn for the upper hall, there was a railed landing. Access was gained to it by a gate from the hall, and it was lighted dimly by a ruby lamp in a lantern hanging by a chain. A big piece of imitation tapestry covered the whole wall space behind it, from ceiling to floor. It had been an "improvement," contrived at the turn of the century; it was in fact nothing but a large clothes closet with the rear wall taken away—the old door, opening into the sitting-room, could be seen behind the tapestry if anybody looked. It could be seen in the sitting-room, too, rather unfortunately extending up above the secretary that now stood against it.

Well, perhaps it did open out the view a little, thought Rena, climbing the stairs; and the legend was that stringed orchestras played on the railed landing in the old days of receptions, no doubt behind palms. It was of no use now, and it was like the rest of the house; something useless and rather ugly had been superimposed everywhere, or almost everywhere, on honest late-Victorian foundations.

Rena climbed to the upper hall, and turned in to the sitting-room. She put her coat and hat away in one of the two tall closets that flanked the built-in bookshelves, and went on back through the bedroom into the little dressing-room beyond it. She had taken off her dress in order to wash for dinner, when the dumb-waiter doors began to rattle—they seemed to catch every draught. They had kept her awake half the night before. She must find something to stuff up the big gap between them, caused no doubt by the warping of the old wood. They were half-doors, coming together with a flimsy bolt.

A couple of circulars might stuff up the crack, or thick letters, or folded newspaper. But when Rena went back through the blue-satin and walnut bedroom to the sitting-room, she found nothing of the kind anywhere. A thin paper-bound book, perhaps? She had seen one or two on those shelves. Here were two thin books, one paper-bound and one in morocco, tied together with faded old pink tape, crushed between *The New Newgate Calendar* and *The Trial of the Stauntons*.

She took them out; very dusty, quite old. The bound book was in half-morocco, red, faded; the paper book was faded too, coloured like dust itself. She came over to the light, laid the bound book on the table and began to clap the pages of the other, holding it well away from her slip.

Gray was coming up the stairs; she stopped, the book open in her hands, while he slowly climbed to the hall and slowly came into the sitting-room. He had her book in his hand, and he threw it aside on the table without looking at her.

"Don't think much of that," he said. Very well then, she wasn't going to inform him that she had met the author. He was always bored when she said anything about her work, anyway.

"I mean," he said, "who cares?"

"It seemed interesting to me."

"Morbid." He glanced then at the open book in her hand; and when he raised his eyes to hers, Rena had never seen such a look on anybody's face before. It was murderous. He snatched the thing out of her hand, looked down and saw the other, snatched that up too. He read the title, which was more than Rena had done. Putting one on top of the other, he raised his eyes again to meet hers.

"Doing a little research?" he asked. One hand fell away to his side, and she saw almost without believing her eyes that it clenched into a fist.

She stepped back. "Gray, what's the matter with you?"

His pale face was flushed now to his forehead. He looked down at the books again, and at her. She was completely terrified.

"Gray, are you going crazy? Why shouldn't I read them? And I wasn't reading them; I don't even know what they're about. I was dusting them."

He swallowed after a moment, and said in a husky voice: "Dusting them?"

"I was going to stuff up the crack in the dumbwaiter doors. You know how it rattles."

After another pause, in a different tone, he said: "No, I don't. I sleep at night."

It was at last too much for her; she said: "Gray, let me go. You don't want me. It isn't as if you really needed me. If you did, I'd stay. But I won't stay now."

If she had been frightened before, that was nothing to what she felt now. He took a step towards her, and the clenched hand at his side rose a little; then he suddenly turned, went out of the room, and slammed the door behind him. She heard the key turn in the lock.

Twice in the last few minutes she had been in actual fear of her life; this was as bad but different; she had never dreamed what it would feel like to be locked up anywhere. There was horror in it. To be helpless, to wait for that door to open again, to see that maniac's face of his—no. All in a moment she was galvanized into action by plain rage.

She looked all round the sitting-room, and her eyes fastened on the foot of disused doorway that showed above the secretary. She ran over and dragged at the side of the secretary—she could hardly move it, but it came out a foot at last. She stood peering in at the old door; the knob had been taken away, and when she put a finger into the big old keyhole and worked the door back and forth a little, or tried to, she was sure it was locked. Those old locks...three closets in the room... three keys?

No; only the closet nearest her had a key in it, a large heavy key. She got it out and tried it in the disused door, and the lock turned; what was more, the door swung open towards her; when the knob was taken out the spring that controlled the hasp must have been weakened. She could put her hand through and feel the smooth reverse of the machine-made tapestry.

She backed around the side of the secretary, whirled, and hurried lightly through to the dressing-room. She knew how little time she had; Gray had gone down to consult his brother and sister, those mysterious little books would be shown them. Then something would be done. But he had locked her in, and left her half-dressed and in a paralysis of fear; he might not think it necessary to hurry back.

She pulled her dress on, came back to the sitting-room and got her coat and hat out of the closet—she mustn't look too crazy on the street. Gloves and handbag she must have left down in the library. No time to look, no time for anything—she must be gone before Gray even thought she would try it.

That other girl, she thought, as she squeezed past the secretary, through the door, between the wall and the tapestry: had she been locked in? A thought followed by another, which seemed to come of itself—had she tried to get out by a window, and fallen, and had they hushed it up and called her death pneumonia? But no, Dr. Wolfram wouldn't—he had been old Mr. Austen's doctor, and he seemed a pleasant sort of man. She might go to him, but he was their doctor now, and it was too late. She knew where he lived, though.

Half-way down the stairs she heard voices in the library; Jerome's, raised in anger: "You obsessed fool, go up there and unlock that door and apologize." But that didn't mean they'd let her go. Well, if they tried to stop her now she could scream and make trouble—the servants would hear. They wouldn't like that.

She reached the front door, left it open behind her, and ran down to the street. Not a minute to lose now, and it seemed so far to the corner. She was half-running. Mr. Ordway and dog, coming along across the way from the direction of the park, saw her and stared. They crossed diagonally and caught up with her.

Ordway asked: "Trouble? Anything I can do?" and did not break his stride.

"I have to go. I have to go."

"Looks like it." He took in her set face from which all the bloom had gone, her fixed grey eyes, the bare hands holding her coat together. No worry here; plain funk, to him.

"You lamming out of there?" he asked as coolly as if such a thing might happen to anybody.

"Don't tell. Please don't tell."

"Tell? Certainly I won't tell. You need a cab."

They had reached the corner; a cab was pulling up in front of the apartment house, the doorman letting someone out of it. She gasped: "I haven't any money for it."

"That's all right, I have cab fare on me." He signalled the driver, who would have gone on home if Rena had been the one to signal him. He waited at the corner while Ordway followed the doorman up to the entrance, passed him Gawain's leash and a dollar bill: "Hold on to this boy for me, will you, George? Back in a minute."

The doorman knew him by sight, accepted the leash and put a finger up to his cap.

Ordway put Rena into the cab and got in himself. She said in a stifled voice: "Just make him drive away."

Ordway leaned forward: "Grab this light up and over to Park, and then we'll tell you." He sat back as the cab swung left. "I'm getting out any time," he explained in his equable way. "Just say the word. You'd better have a five in ones, wouldn't you think so?"

"I don't know—can't explain." She was barely able to talk.

"You don't have to. Seen you on the block lots of times," said Ordway. "Quiet type, minding your own business and being good to the old pup. I feel as if we were old friends. I feel as if you knew what you were about, and wouldn't run off just for the fun of it."

"Oh, it was too much. I had to go. I was too frightened."

"No good sticking around and doing nothing if you're frightened," said Ordway. "Better to run one way or the other. I've done it dozens of times."

The cab stopped at Park Avenue for the lights, and the driver looked around. Rena gave him an address.

If you're curious about other books in
Felony & Mayhem's "Vintage"
category, here is the first chapter of
the forthcoming title *The Glass Mask*,
by Lenore Glen Offord

CHAPTER ONE

TODD MCKINNON'S CAR could easily have done seventy miles an hour on this broad and tempting road down the Sacramento Valley, but wartime restrictions held its speed to a sedate thirty-five. The spring-green curves of hill rising on either side of the road seemed never to change from one mile to the next.

There were three silent persons in the front seat of the car, each subduing his own particular brand of impatience. Todd was exercising rigid control over the foot that rested so lightly on the accelerator, and thinking longingly of letting her out. Georgine Wyeth, beside him, could almost sense this emotion through the shoulder which companionably touched hers, although what could be seen of his face under the tilt of his soft hat betrayed no visible strain. The flat plane of cheek, the sharply cut jaw and firm mouth with its glint of sandy mustache, added up to their usual sum of impassive good nature. She hoped her own appearance was as relaxed. The one thing she wanted was to get home as soon as possible after one of the most exhausting days she could remember.

Todd glanced beyond her at her daughter Barby, wedged in by the window, and then met Georgine's eyes in amusement. The child's slender little nape, framed in tow-colored pigtails, was still tense with excitement, bliss, and the desire to talk.

This had been Barby's day. She was exactly eight years old, and the celebration, specified by herself, had embraced not only a day off from school but a visit to the army camp at Sacramento where Todd's eldest nephew was stationed. Sergeant Dyke McKinnon, twenty-one years old, was a redheaded charmer and well used to making rapid conquests; but Barby's instant adoration, when he had first spent a weekend leave in Berkeley, had been of a character to turn any man's head. To most adults she seemed a plain, silent child, with a remote gravity that was very nearly formidable. When she got one of her rare crushes she lit up like a pinball game. The sergeant, who had small sisters of his own, had fallen with an almost audible thud.

Barby's silence for the past half hour was not from choice. For the first few miles out of Sacramento she had jabbered so incessantly that she was now under orders not to speak again until she had counted five large red objects, nothing smaller than a motorcycle accepted. Therefore, Barby's eyes were now diligently searching the countryside. She was dressed in a miniature WAVES hat and coat, her birthday gift from Todd. In one hand she clutched a flashlight, her favorite among Dyke's lavish assortment of presents. Georgine thought, I must remember this; it's something to have seen a perfectly happy person.

Todd McKinnon said, after a glance at his watch, "H'm, nearly five-thirty. What do you think, Georgine? Shall we stop off for a minute to see those friends of Dyke's?"

"What friends?" Georgine said hazily. She had only the vaguest memory of the sergeant's parting words, something about a girl and her charming aunt.

"They live at Valleyville. We'd have to turn off the main highway for a few miles."

"Isn't it a bit late for a call? And when we're eager to get home—"

"I've been figuring. We'd have to stop somewhere for supper, it'll be after seven before we get to Berkeley—at this rate of speed," Mr. McKinnon put in with venomous inflection. "We might as well drop in at this place for a fifteen-minute call, and then be on our way again. Wouldn't lose much time."

It was an effort to make decisions, but Georgine considered the plan. "On the whole, I should think not," she began.

"And a red barn and a red house," Barby shrieked. "That's five. Now can I talk, Mamma? Look, we haff to stop in that town Cousin Dyke told us about. We *haff* to."

"No, we don't, darling. What makes you think that?"

"Well, it was the very last thing he said, to stop there on our way home if we got a chance because his girlfriend lived there, and if she wasn't home her aunt would be, and he thought Toddy would be interested."

"But that was only if we felt like it, Barby, and we're all tired. You've been running your legs off since eight this morning. I think we'd better go straight home."

Barby said nothing, but her chin went in slowly and she looked at the floor of the car. The back of her neck was completely heartrending.

Todd and Georgine exchanged a swift look. Georgine thought, *Oh, dear, I'm spoiling her.* I'm going to be one of those soft fools who can't refuse her child anything... Just the same, it was evident that the glory had gone out of the day for Barby, and Barby's mother couldn't bear it.

"Then let's turn off and stop in Valleyville," she said swiftly. Barby's head came up, and the radiance returned to her face. "If it means so much to you, darling. I can't quite see why you want to stop there."

"Well, because Cousin Dyke said to."

"'Whereon thy feet have trod,'" Georgine murmured. "Thank heaven you asked me for a doll, anyway."

Mr. McKinnon chuckled quietly to himself, and swung the car to the right. He thought, How easy it is to make a child happy. Why do we ever hesitate?

It was an enchanting small town. Georgine didn't know quite what she had been expecting; perhaps only the nice, undistinguished white or buff stucco of the newer valley towns; but she had not visualized anything like this gentle period piece, its cottages and narrow two-story frame houses set sociably close to each other and to the streets, its lilac bushes springing from neatly kept lawns, its huge trees, newly green with the approach of April, arching the pavement. She thought it must resemble New England. And how exactly like those early settlers in the seventies and eighties, with a whole broad valley to build in, to crowd their houses together in the smallest possible space! Just the same, there was something inexpressibly cozy about it, like a Victorian sitting room.

Todd seemed to be talking to himself. "The end of Walnut Street, wasn't that what he said? The last old house, and the biggest."

"Great heavens, Todd," said Georgine, leaning forward as the car stopped, "it's the town mansion!"

"Or was," McKinnon amended. He shut off the ignition and turned for a good look. "Suffering cats," he added.

There it stood, what remained of a magnificent monstrosity of the eighties; weathered white paint on boards, faded dark green paint on old-fashioned hinged shutters; a flight of front steps worthy of a summer hotel; a front door surrounded with colored panes of glass; corners truncated and then enlarged into square bay windows; tottering upper porches, and dim side porches, and porches inexplicably surrounding the whole third story. The house towered incredibly past the skyline of the enclosing hills, and on every possible inch of its surface there was, or had been, wooden lace.

Todd said he would spy out the land, and left them sitting in the car while he ascended the impressive front steps. Georgine watched him with frank pleasure. She thought, These slim, narrowly built men seem to be hard-surfaced, dust doesn't stick to them and their clothes don't wrinkle... If we're going to pay a call I'd better put on some powder and lipstick. There, the door's opening; I hoped there wouldn't be anybody home.

When she looked up from her mirror Todd was still standing in the doorway talking, his back to her. She glanced once more along the façade of the old house. That stuff at the lower windows must be Nottingham lace. Quite nice plain net or scrim curtained the second floor. There were no curtains at all for the third story, set back a little behind its railed balcony, but the windows were shining clean. The afternoon sun slanted into them just enough so that she could see some object, white or light colored, near the window. Was it someone standing very still, looking down at the car? Nothing was visible but the curve of a shoulder.

"Mamma," Barby said, "lookit across the street, there's a chimney standing up all by itself in the middle of that lot."

"Maybe somebody's house burned down. Some of those trees on the edge of the lot are still brown, it couldn't have been so very long ago." Georgine's eyes returned, after this brief interruption, to the uncurtained windows. The person was still there, unmoving.

Todd came running down the steps. "Young Mrs. Crane isn't home," he said from the sidewalk, "but her aunt Mrs. Peabody is. She very much wants us to come in. Okay for a few minutes?"

"I'll admit I'd love to see the inside of that place," Georgine murmured. "Come on, Barby, at least you can put your feet where Cousin Dyke's have stood."

She observed as they approached the steps that this house boasted a broader side yard than any other on the street. There was some distance between it and the nearest dwelling to the north, a space taken up by a tangle of garden and some dilapidated wooden outbuildings, to which a weedy carriage

drive led from the street. The south side was enclosed by a
line of beautiful maples, old and huge, their branches sweeping
downward like willows. They made an effective screen for
those side windows, Georgine thought, but the lower rooms
must be very dark with all that shade. The porch creaked a
little as she and Todd and Barby crossed it. She reflected that
nothing took on the look and feel and smell of age as wood did;
even outdoors her nostrils caught its sweetish scent.

"Mrs. Peabody went to take off her apron," Todd said in her
ear. "She'll be right out to meet us." The three of them crossed
the threshold, and met an even more perceptible odor of the
Victorian: carpets that had been swept with tea leaves and
wet newspaper, old fabric hangings and furniture polish, and
wood again; but there was also a fragrance of hyacinth from a
bowl on the table, and a hint of baking cookies, and the hall
that stretched before them, nearly the depth of the house, was
exquisitely clean. The slanting sun illuminated it. There were
double doors on the right, a single one on the left, and in the
depths of the hall more doors; at least three of them.

"Oh, lovely," Georgine said under her breath, looking at the
staircase. It was on the right of the hall, starting halfway back,
and rose in a beautiful, flying curve through the high ceiling.

One of the doors at the rear opened, and a small slim
woman came hurrying through. "But I'm so pleased that you
would come in," she was saying, both hands outstretched to
Georgine and Barby. "I can't tell you how much pleasure it
gives me to meet Sergeant McKinnon's family."

Georgine took her in with a quick glance as Todd
performed introductions. Mrs. Peabody must be in her late
thirties, but her sort of attractiveness did not depend on youth.
She had the only really heart-shaped face Georgine had ever
seen, its widely set gray eyes and delicate hollows under the
high cheekbones giving her a look of great sweetness. Georgine
thought, *She plays it up well too; that soft bang cut to a point
in the middle of her forehead. That dress is homemade, but it
fits her perfectly…and how nice of her to shake hands with*

Barby in that grown-up way.

She held her breath for a moment. Normally at such a time Barby, though mannerly, turned into an unresponsive clod of childhood; but this time some of the magic must still be about her. Barby held out a paw which her mother devoutly hoped was not sticky. "How do you do," she said carefully, and added in an awed tone, "Do you know our Cousin Dyke?"

"Yes, I do. He was here to dinner once, and stayed the night."

"Oh, isn't he a lovely man?" Barby said, her voice faint with emotion. "He took me for *a ride in a jeep.*"

"Why, you darling," said Mrs. Peabody under her breath. "When was that, today? I must hear all about it. Come into the sitting room, won't you all?" She gave the adults a brief conspiratorial smile, and opened the door to the left.

Everything about this house seemed to provoke exclamations, either of joy or horror. Georgine sank down on a red plush chair, buttoned into rigid hillocks. For a minute she averted her eyes from the fireplace with its mantelpiece and surround of tortured golden oak, wondering how on earth the same person who had put in that heavenly stair-rail could have tolerated this room: the bamboo table, the jar of pampas grass in the corner—if there was one thing she hated, it was pampas grass!—the woolly chromos on figured wallpaper and the Nottingham lace. Would it be safe to look at Todd?

She glanced at him where he still stood in the doorway, and received a small tingling shock. He was motionless; his eyes were fixed on the fireplace, but he wasn't seeing it. His face, his whole body, wore an attentive look with which she was very familiar. To herself, she called it, "Todd with his aerial extended."

He caught her eye, smiled and came to sit near her. "So," Georgine said in an undertone, "George Washington slept here, too. I wonder if there's a home in the whole Sacramento Valley that hasn't entertained Dyke?"

"The boy gets around," Todd replied absently. "What's he got that I haven't?"

"Nothing," said Georgine. "That's what worries me sometimes." She looked at him speculatively. Two clichés in one breath was too high an average for Todd; there was no doubt of it, he was preoccupied with something more than the fascinating horrors of the room. His eyes kept resting on one bit of furniture after another, as if he were trying to remember something.

"And we met a lot of soldiers, Cousin Dyke knows them all," said Barby, seated on a sofa beside Mrs. Peabody. "Some of them wanted to buy me Popsicles, too, but Mamma wouldn't let 'em."

"I should think not," Georgine remarked. "I had my hands full with Dyke alone." She felt almost dizzy herself, thinking of the milk shakes, popcorn and candy bars pressed on her daughter by the infatuated sergeant; but Barby's cheeks were healthily colored, perhaps she was not going to be sick after all.

"We're in perfect agreement about your nephew, Mr. McKinnon," Mrs. Peabody said. "He really is charming. I can see that Mary Helen—that's Mrs. Crane—has some dangerous competition here."

The conversation became general, full of pleasant nothings to which Georgine could contribute without real attention. She glanced at an amazing marble clock which ornamented the mantel; in about three minutes one could decently suggest leaving...

"Oh, no, you *mustn't*," said Mrs. Peabody. "Couldn't you stay just for a pick-up supper? It would be such a pleasure to me, I don't really expect the children tonight and it does get very lonely for me, eating by myself."

She was alone, then? There hadn't been another member of the household on the third floor, looking at the car that had driven up?

Georgine made one more effort. "Truly, we must be getting on. It's so hospitable of you, Mrs. Peabody, but it's been a long day—and anyway, I don't see how Barby could eat anything."

"Well, I think I could. Bread and butter, and meat and potatoes, things like that," said Barby carefully.

I ruined my case with that last remark, thought Georgine despairingly. Now we'll never get away; she acts as if she really wanted us to stay, and Todd would like to, I know.

"It won't take a minute," Mrs. Peabody said with real pleasure, getting up and moving toward the rear of the house. "I have some chicken I canned myself last summer, so if you'll just entertain yourselves for a few minutes—no, no, of course you're not to help, Mrs. Wyeth! Won't you just rest, or look around if you care to?" Her voice floated back to them through the adjoining dining room, and was lost as a door closed.

Immediately Todd said, "Barby, play a game with me, will you? Go stand in the dining room, facing me, and don't tell me what you see; let me tell you."

Barby complied, interested and quietly giggling.

"Is there," said Todd portentously, "on each side of that archway which I can't see through from here—is there a whatnot?"

"What's a whatnot?"

"A sort of cabinet made of open shelves. You see them? H'm. Is there a picture hanging up over each one—a very cross-looking gentleman on the left, and a pie-faced lady on the right?"

Barby looked at her hands, figuring out which was which, and then nodded delightedly.

"Has one of the whatnots got a huge shell sitting on it? And do the shelves have bobbles hanging along the edges?"

"Yes. How'd you know that, Toddy? I didn't see you come in here. Have you been here before?"

"No," Todd said, "that I know for sure. I only feel as if I had."

"Darling, that just means your brain has fallen in half, or something like that." Georgine grinned at him.

"Maybe. Thanks, cricket, you can come in now. The game's over." He got up and began prowling with his light step about the room. His deep-set gray eyes were narrowed against the level evening light, and he bit his lip reflectively. "No, Georgine, this is something more than the I-have-been-here-before feeling. That only lasts a minute. I might have deduced the whatnots, but I've really seen that shell somewhere, and the portraits. I knew it as soon as we stepped into the house, though I wasn't sure until I saw the mantelpiece." His lean face looked actually troubled. "It's like something that oughtn't to be familiar, and yet is; as if—well, damn it, as if I were in Fall River, and walked down Second Street and went into a totally undistinguished house, and everything in it had been left the same for fifty-one years."

His glance at Barby, now quietly sitting in the upholstered niche of the bay window, seemed to say that he couldn't elucidate now. Georgine knew she ought to remember something about Fall River, but what it was eluded her.

She closed her eyes. This was rather pleasant; once having overcome her reluctance to impose on a stranger, she had to admit that it was better than getting home late and cooking supper in a tired hurry—certainly better than a crowded restaurant. Perhaps she could get Todd to leave before eight. He was sweet with Barby, as solicitous about her care as if he were already her stepfather.

"Bless her heart," said Mrs. Peabody's soft voice, "I believe she's gone to sleep sitting up."

Georgine opened her eyes to deny it, but saw that her daughter was the one referred to. Barby had indeed gone to sleep, as suddenly and deeply as if she'd been drugged. The WAVES hat was tilted at a drunken angle over one ear, and her feet dangled appealingly from the window seat, but she still had her flashlight in one hand.

"Let's not wake her," Georgine said, struggling to her feet. "She's really had enough to eat today. Right after supper, if you'll forgive us, Mrs. Peabody, we'll get her home."

They closed the sliding doors between dining room and sitting room, and sat down at one end of an immense old walnut table. Mrs. Peabody's cooking was quite as appetizing as her personal appearance, and under the stimulus of food and hot coffee Georgine found herself having an extremely good time. What a nice woman, she thought more than once; so gentle, but with that crisp little sense of comedy.

She and her hostess swapped anecdotes of wartime shopping, with much laughter; Mrs. Peabody praised Georgine's child with exactly the right amount of warmth, doing herself no harm in the mother's eyes; after a time Todd, no longer preoccupied, gave a masterly description of the battle at El Alamein, illustrating with tableware and using a bread tray for the Qattara Depression. "Do you smoke?" Mrs. Peabody asked. "Oh, please do, I'd enjoy it myself but I mustn't, on account of a silly heart condition." The room swam into a pleasant haze of candlelight and drifting wreaths of smoke; Georgine could see the three of them reflected in the mirror of a massive buffet that stood at right angles to the windows.

"Now, I'm really afraid that we—" Georgine began at last; and at almost the same moment Mrs. Peabody turned to glance at the windows. "Oh! It's *dark*!" she said abruptly, in an unsteady voice.

The sweet hollows below her cheekbones seemed to deepen, and for a moment her eyes were filled with apprehension. Georgine thought, Here's another poor gal who's afraid of the dark; but I hope I never show it as obviously as that.

"Isn't it foolish of me," said Nella Peabody, and for a moment clasped her hands in a curiously appealing gesture, "but I—I have a quite unfounded dislike of being alone here. An old house seems so very large at night, don't you think? It begins to settle and creak as soon as the air cools, and I can always imagine... Oh, I really do wish the family had consented to my making this into a tourist home, I'd always thought it would be a good plan, there are those five bedrooms upstairs if you count the little sewing room—but I rather gave up the plan when the highway was cut off, and then afterward Mary Helen and Horace wanted to come and live here, so it seemed best to keep it in the family. But they're not here much. Horace is part owner of our drugstore, and his hours are very peculiar, and he's like as not to be so keyed up after work that he'll thumb a ride to Vallejo or some town that's wide open all night for the shipyard people, and not get home until after breakfast. And Mary Helen has friends—If they only stayed all the time, if I could count on them—but to be here *alone...* "

She looked down at her hands, pressing tighter and tighter together. She unloosed them, with an effort, and laughed shakily. "I'm babbling. Please forgive me, I didn't mean to inflict my foolishness on you. Will you open the folding doors for me, Mr. McKinnon?"

Todd had said nothing, but stood looking at her with his peculiar air of attention. Now, as he slid the doors apart, he glanced once more about the sitting room, whose appalling furniture seemed to start out and then retreat from the candlelight. Georgine saw him shake his head almost imperceptibly. She thought, It's almost as if he knew that Mrs. Peabody was afraid of something definite instead of just plain being scared the way I am, alone in the dark.

"Still dead to the world," he said, laying a gentle hand on Barby's cheek.

"Does she feel hot, Todd?"

"No, just normal. I suppose I'd better get the robe out of the car to wrap her in?"

Mrs. Peabody switched on a lamp, shaded with a huge globe of painted glass. "It seems almost dangerous to take her out in the night air, after she's been warm under that afghan," she said quietly. "I—I don't suppose you'd consent to stay overnight?"

Georgine felt as if she'd seen this coming, a long way back; as if something had been settled, hours ago, without reference to any of the three adults who now stood looking at each other before the dim cavern of the dining room. Even as the words of refusal shaped themselves in her mind, she could hear how futile, how petty they would sound.

"It's almost as if you were in the family," Mrs. Peabody was saying, with that attractive smile. "And I'd like to see a little more of you. I'd be so—so *grateful* if you'd stay."

Georgine thought queerly, They're all against me: Mrs. Peabody, and Barby—it was true that sudden changes in temperature sometimes brought back remnants of Barby's asthma, which she had battled for so many years—and Todd. Todd wanted to stay, she knew with a sixth sense, and his quiet face confirmed it when she glanced at him. There was nothing to set up against the three except her own selfish wishes.

She made the sounds anyway, but she was beaten before she started. There wasn't even the problem of nightgowns and toothbrushes. To get an early start on the wonderful day with Dyke, they had driven to Sacramento the night before, and stayed at a hotel.

Mrs. Peabody mustn't go to the least trouble, she heard herself saying weakly. She must be allowed to help her hostess with the dishes, and to make up the beds for the three of them. Well, no, Barby wasn't used to sleeping with anyone, but for one night—oh, if there was a cot which could be set up without too much fuss, that would be perfect.

She felt Todd's eyes, amused and loving, resting on her during this highly feminine conversation. Luckily he was one of those men who like women to be themselves. She grinned at him now, mutely apologizing for all this flutter, and asked if, after he'd put the car away in that shed at the rear, he'd stay with Barby and wake her by gentle degrees.

"Don't be surprised if you find some dust upstairs," said Nella Peabody cheerfully, climbing the soaring flight with one hand on the rail. "I don't get up more than once or twice a day, on doctor's orders. Luckily there was a maid's room downstairs with a lavatory attached, that I could take for my own after— after my husband went to war." She said the last words quickly, resolutely. It was her first mention of her own circumstances, Georgine realized with some surprise. "Oh, by the way," Mrs. Peabody went on, stopping a few steps from the top, "are you by any chance afraid of rats?"

"Yes," said Georgine in a horrified whisper.

"Oh, please don't look like that, we never see them. They never leave the attic, I promise you. Nobody's ever seen them up there, as it happens, nor even caught one in a trap—though not for want of trying. I just wanted to warn you you might hear them; at least, that's what the children say makes the pattering and rustling noises upstairs. They don't mind it in the least, they tell me."

"Then I mustn't either," said Georgine grimly. They crossed a shadowy upper hall, wide with the splendid wastefulness of space favored by architects of the past century, and, like the one downstairs, walled with doors and doors and doors.

"I'll put you and the little girl in here," said Mrs. Peabody, opening the door of a large room on the front corner and flipping a wall switch. Georgine looked in, and felt her eyes widening in sheer amazement.

She had the third tiny, undefined shock of the last few hours. The hall was furnished with more buttoned plush chairs and hung with yet more chromos. Coming out of it into this room was like stepping from one century into another. There was a plain broadloom rug; there was a good, ordinary bedroom suite of double bed, vanity and chest and chair and bed table, certainly bought within the past few years. It was more than an anachronism; in some mysterious way it was almost an insult to the eyes.

Mrs. Peabody must have read her thoughts or her expression. "It was the only one we did over. Most of the rest of the house is just dreadful, of course, and we'd meant to get at that too when we could afford it; but of course I shouldn't think of touching it until Gilbert comes home. There isn't going to be one thing different," she said fiercely, as if challenged, and gave her dark head a little shake. In the next moment she was all business. "The cot is right here, in the sewing room." She opened a door which Georgine had thought led to a closet and disclosed a small room built across the front of the hall. "Oh, no, it isn't. We must have taken it up attic, the last time I made Mary Helen a dress; it's so seldom I really get around up here. I'll go up and make sure."

"Among the rats?" Georgine inquired, with an attempt at laughter.

"My dear, I keep telling you they never appear... No, certainly I won't try to get it down alone, I'd just better make sure before we call Mr. McKinnon."

"I'll come too. If it's one of those Army cots I could get it myself." She caught the relieved expression in her hostess' eyes, and they both began to laugh.

"You can't imagine, my dear," said Mrs. Peabody earnestly, "how much good it does me to find somebody who's scared of the same things I am."

"I'm determined I'm going to break myself of being a coward." Georgine followed her into the hall. "I might as well, I can't show it in front of Barby anyway. She is *not* going to grow up the way I did, afraid of thunderstorms and snakes and burglars, without any foundation. With any luck, she'll never find me out."

Mrs. Peabody opened one of the numerous doors, midway on the side of the hall opposite the guest room. It gave on a sort of entry in which mops and brooms were visible; beyond them were uncarpeted stairs, going both up and down, and protected by banisters which, Georgine saw with amusement, were as elaborate in their gingerbread trimmings as the outside of the house. A yellowish bulb partly illuminated both flights and the closetlike entry. Mrs. Peabody, beginning to climb with her usual caution, remarked that there was a better light at the top.

"And now," she added, pausing for breath, as the stairs debouched into a large attic with a skylight, "I imagine Susan Labaré will be over tomorrow, if she doesn't telephone tonight, to ask if we've had prowlers in the attic. She's thought so once or twice before, and it took all three of us to convince her that the moon on the skylight gave exactly the effect of a light in this room!" She turned on a blue-white bulb by the stairs, as she spoke; her eyes darted quickly from side to side of the big irregular space.

Georgine afterward confessed to herself that she didn't know what she had expected to find. Logic told her that there could scarcely be a mad relation kept chained up here, like Rochester's wife, but that figure by the window had stayed in her memory. Now she saw dangling from a hook in a rafter a large chintz dress bag with a zipper. Its top was curved in hanger shape, or like the slope of a shoulder, and it was beside one of the front windows.

"Forgive my laughing to myself," she said, lugging the camp cot down the stairs. "It's about something so silly I couldn't even put it into words."

Strange house or no strange house, she was so tired that once in bed she was asleep in a few minutes. In that short time a succession of talking pictures flicked through her mind: Barby, still two-thirds asleep, tottering up the front stairs—"You don't haff to carry me. It's just babies that get carried. Mamma said when I was eight I wasn't a baby any more. She said I could get up and go to the bathroom at night by myself, if had to, and I'm going to, because I've got my flashlight." Nella Peabody, scrubbing away at the dishes with delicate thoroughness, chatting with such apparent freedom and yet letting fall so little about herself—"What a charming man Mr. McKinnon is, if you don't mind my saying so. I do like the way his face—how shall I put it?—comes alive when he looks at you." Todd himself, saying good night at the top of the stairs; "comes alive" was a very good way of describing what happened to his face when he was relaxed or interested. The day at the army camp had been hard on him; it must have been; all those men, some of them older and less healthy-looking than he, in uniform. A flattened lung didn't show. It was hard on him, but wasn't she glad of it for herself!…He had something new to think of, in this hospitable house—had anyone in pioneer days ever asked strangers to "'light and set" more cordially than Nella Peabody had invited them into her home? "I'm so grateful to you for staying," she had said.

Just before she fell asleep, Georgine thought of what it was that had happened in Fall River, Massachusetts, in 1892.

She woke only once. The moon, a night or two past its full, poured light through the angled bay window; that must have been what awakened her, for the sounds in the garret were barely perceptible. Pattering, scraping, now and then a little rattling shower as if bits of plaster had fallen. Georgine, burrowing deeper into bed, hoped it was true that nobody ever saw the rats. She wondered drowsily what it was they did that sounded like tapping, very far off but regular. It was true that the old house creaked and cracked alarmingly as its atmosphere grew cooler. She was glad she knew the reason for it, because those sounds could not be laid to the rats, nor could the impression that she had heard a door closing somewhere below.

She was also glad, the next morning, that she hadn't let herself imagine anything sinister, for it was plain that at some time during the night one of the other occupants of the house had arrived. Georgine saw him, to their shared surprise, in the hall: a tall youngish man, his blond hair in a mat of dishevelment, lightly clad in the lower half of his pajamas and just emerging from the bathroom. "Great God!" the man exclaimed, peering nearsightedly at the open door of her room; and then bolted incontinently across the hall to disappear behind one of those other doors.

Georgine had clutched her dark silk robe more tightly around her at this vision, but was moved more to laughter than to horror. That must be Horace, whom Mrs. Peabody had mentioned; what was he, her nephew, cousin, or what? She spoke of him as part of "the family." Well, if Horace never let his aunt know when he was coming home, it served him right to be confronted by strange women.

Horace's door opened a crack, though he remained invisible. From behind it his voice came, an oddly soft and breathy voice that made his words all the more apologetic. "I do beg your pardon, but I just got in and I didn't know anyone was here. Should I—uh—have we met?"

"No," said Georgine, stopping halfway across the hall to laugh silently.

Horace seemed to be communing with himself. "I know I'm in the right house," he said tentatively.

"You are. Don't worry, we're just overnight guests."

"Well, as long as I didn't startle *you* too much. I thought I was having a bad dream," said the voice chattily. "Not that you look like a nightmare, God knows, but to see somebody coming out of *that* room—"

Georgine shut the bathroom door behind her without answering. Horace, she thought, might not be quite sober; or perhaps his night duty at the drugstore made him lightheaded.

When she returned Barby was up, bristling with energy after a fourteen-hour sleep. She jigged from one foot to the other as Georgine attempted to braid her hair and button her dress. "Mamma, this is fun! Just think, night before last we stayed at a hotel and last night we stayed here, I wish we didn't ever have to go back home."

"I don't," said her mother, brushing vigorously.

"Well, I guess I'd like to be back for Betty Dillman's birthday party, but I love it when we go on travels like this. Mamma, where'd Toddy sleep? Can I go and wake him up, if he's right down the hall? Listen, Mamma, when I kiss Toddy I pick out that little smooth spot right under his eye, if I try anywhere else his whiskers prickle me. Don't they ever prickle you?"

"Sometimes, but I don't seem to mind it," said Georgine. "And those aren't whiskers—stand *still*, Barby!—that's a neat military mustache."

Barby thought this was very funny. She was still giggling ecstatically as they started down for breakfast. Georgine should have noticed that she was a little above herself, but her attention was diverted by the sight of an entire pound of butter furnishing forth the breakfast table. "You mustn't!" she said reprovingly to Mrs. Peabody. "All those points! Luckily we brought our ration books, we'll—"

"No, you won't," said Mrs. Peabody briskly. "The judge sends me butter from the farm, and chickens and vegetables too. It's fun to be able to share them. I have the children's food stamps, too, and they eat so few meals here—Good morning, Mr. McKinnon, I do hope you're hungry."

Todd, coming quietly in and smiling at the three ladies, said that he was. And yes, he had slept well, and no, he had not heard any rats; it took more than that to waken him; an earthquake, say.

"Toddy," Barby squeaked happily, "did your brain come back together again?"

"That was a figure of speech, Barby," said Georgine repressively; but their hostess looked an astonished question.

"I had the feeling that I'd been here before; I had it last night, and Barby heard me mention it," Todd said with an odd gravity. He inquired if there was any news in the paper, and applied himself to his breakfast. Sunlight came through the new-leaved vines over the kitchen window, and spattered on the shining nickel of the percolator. Nella Peabody said how becoming that orchid cotton print was to Barby's fairness; had her mother ever thought of a deeper, bluer shade, almost violet? No, indeed, it wouldn't be too old for her. Mrs. Peabody had a lovely piece of challis that had been meant for a little girl's dress, but the parents had changed their minds. "I just love to sew for little girls," she added, smiling at her youngest guest. Barby looked at her mother with a slow dawn of hope, she adored new clothes, and heaven knew she didn't have many; but Georgine had to shake her head, and see the radiant look die out slowly.

"There's nothing we'd like better than to have you make something for her, if we were staying here, Mrs. Peabody," she said, "but you know we must be starting home in an hour or so. No, darling, don't even ask to stay. We mustn't argue, you've talked plenty this morning already."

"I was just talkin' to myself, then," Barby said. "Toddy does that, he was doing it last night when I woke up. Was I in bed? Where was I when I heard him? You know what you said, Toddy? You said somepin' about had a lie, 'n tells it. Who had a lie?"

At this seeming irrelevance Georgine was surprised to see Todd's lips tighten. He glanced at his hostess. She had turned off the spigot of the percolator, though his cup underneath it was only half full, and was returning his look intently, her eyes wide, her breast rising and falling with uneven breaths.

"Adeline Tillsit," said Mrs. Peabody softly. "That was what you said, wasn't it? You've heard her name, then? It meant something to you?"

It was a minute before he spoke. "Yes, I've heard her name," he said in that casual voice that was so restful, so unexcited. "She was very old when she died, wasn't she? And this house was a showplace in its day. I remembered why I had thought I'd been here before; one of my newspaper friends had a full set of photographs that were taken—while she was still alive. They'd planned to run a feature story on it some time: famous belle of the eighties, that sort of thing; but I believe the war pictures rather crowded it out."

"Yes," Mrs. Peabody said, with a quiet that matched his, "she died on the same weekend that France fell. That was why there was no publicity at all; we were spared that, because nobody outside of town heard much about it. In the old days, it would have made a—a small sensation, let's say, but the reporters from the city papers were too busy just then to follow it up."

Barby asked for another muffin.

"May I ask," said Mrs. Peabody, breathing a bit more rapidly, "when you saw those photographs? Was it before or after she died?"

"After," Todd said.

"Then perhaps you heard that she was supposed to have been—m-u-r-d-e-r-e-d?" Mrs. Peabody spelled rapidly.